As If by Magic

Also by

EDGARD TELLES RIBEIRO

The Impostor

As If by Magic

Edgard Telles Ribeiro

Translated from the Portuguese by
Kim M. Hastings and Margaret A. Neves

Bellevue Literary Press
NEW YORK

First published in the United States in 2026

For information, contact:
Bellevue Literary Press
90 Broad Street
Suite 2100
New York, NY 10004
www.blpress.org

"Remains from the Fair," "Albatross," and "Turn of the River" were previously published in Portuguese as *No coração da floresta* by Editoria Record.

"The Magic Eye" was previously published in Portuguese as *Jogo de armar* by Todavia.

The English translation of "Albatross" first appeared in Electric Literature's *Recommended Reading*, and the English translation of "Remains from the Fair" first appeared in the *Pittsburgh Review of Books*.

Library of Congress Cataloging-in-Publication Data

Names: Telles Ribeiro, Edgard, author. | Hastings, Kim M., translator. | Neves, Margaret A., translator. | Telles Ribeiro, Edgard. No coração da floresta. English. | Telles Ribeiro, Edgard. Jogo de armar. English.
Title: As if by magic / Edgard Telles Ribeiro ; translated from the Portuguese by Kim M. Hastings and Margaret A. Neves.
Description: First edition. | New York : Bellevue Literary Press, 2026.
Identifiers: LCCN 2025006980 | ISBN 9781954276505 (paperback ; acid-free paper) | ISBN 9781954276512 (epub)
Subjects: LCGFT: Fiction.
Classification: LCC PQ9698.28.I1547 A913 2026 | DDC 869.3/42--dc23/eng/20250311
LC record available at https://lccn.loc.gov/2025006980

Bellevue Literary Press would like to thank all its generous donors—individuals and foundations—for their support.

This publication is made possible by the New York State Council on the Arts with the support of the Office of the Governor and the New York State Legislature.

Book design and composition by Mulberry Tree Press, Inc.

Bellevue Literary Press is committed to ecological stewardship in our book production practices, working to reduce our impact on the natural environment.

♾ This book is printed on acid-free paper.

Manufactured in the United States of America.

First Edition

10 9 8 7 6 5 4 3 2 1

paperback ISBN: 978-1-954276-50-5
ebook ISBN: 978-1-954276-51-2

For my wife, Angelica

Contents

As If by Magic

Remains from the Fair

At the time my father began to suffer from Alzheimer's disease, I didn't realize at first he was confusing things a little. At most, I noticed that he became somewhat repetitive in his gestures and personal routines. I was also aware that he had started dressing with a certain flair. This was new, considering his habits, which were generally frugal.

But for all practical purposes, he continued to lead an outwardly normal life. Although retired, he still helped out a few clients whose interests he had defended for years on end when he practiced law at one of the most respected firms in Rio de Janeiro. He drove his own car, kept his bank account in order, and was a member of a well-known golf club; neither these nor any other activities brought obvious signs of difficulty to the surface. Yet the changes were taking place, steadily, if almost imperceptibly.

He lived alone except for an old servant named Marta. The formality that prevailed between them had also prevented this zealous woman from detecting variations in his behavior.

Then, a few months ago, my father had appeared in the kitchen of his apartment, wearing a dark wool suit and carrying a small suitcase. He announced he would not be home for dinner, and would be absent for two days.

Marta didn't find anything unusual in this; my father did

travel with a certain regularity on short business trips, which often came up at the last minute. But when he returned less than an hour later without the suitcase, his hair mussed and his clothes wrinkled, she couldn't hide her surprise. She was clearly under the impression that he had been mugged.

Very cautiously, she asked him some questions, to which he made vague replies as he drank a glass of water. The minute he left the kitchen, she called me. Considering her words carefully, she described what had happened. Before hanging up, she suggested I stop by to take a look at Dad.

I immediately went to visit him. Since my mother's death, I have gone regularly to the apartment in Laranjeiras, where he has lived for over thirty years, and where I myself spent the end of my adolescence. We usually discuss the events of the day and watch the news on television. We almost always share a meal, each dealing in his own way with the empty seat at the head of the table. After coffee, invariably served on the small terrace, he accompanies me to the entrance hall of the building. Weather permitting, we walk to the square at the end of the street.

That night, I found him adjusting the living room curtains, which he closed after a quick glance at the windows of the building across the street. He had combed his hair and taken off his suit jacket but was still wearing a tie, vest, and suspenders. He approached me and put a hand rather solemnly on my shoulder. But when he opened his mouth, it was to tell me something that seemed completely out of tune with the inner flow of his thoughts. He announced he had just returned from a small rural town, which he didn't name.

Casually, I inquired about his trip. By way of an answer, he complained of the bus, the bumpy roads, and the uncomfortable hotel where he had spent two nights. But he didn't say where he had been.

I accepted his invitation for dinner. Between soup and dessert, I didn't notice anything unusual in his behavior, except that he made several little balls with the soft part of the bread and then lined them up in three precise rows on the tablecloth. He had evidently withdrawn into himself, and this was odd. As we talked, he continued to avoid my references to his absence, which he merely alluded to as "unexpected business."

In the days following, I made it a point to telephone him several times. During one of our conversations, I noticed that his sentences weren't altogether clear—and that he seemed irritated with himself. He described an episode that had distressed him. He had arranged to meet some friends for lunch at a restaurant they had frequented for years. At the appointed time, however, he couldn't locate the place.

In recent months, a series of construction sites have turned the center of the city upside down, making access to certain streets difficult. In his eyes, however, this fact didn't justify the misfortune to which he had fallen victim—especially since the area where he had gotten lost was close to his old office.

The more he crisscrossed the streets of the block, the farther he got from his destination. He even asked passersby for directions, but their instructions only accentuated his sense of helplessness. At one point he had closed his eyes, trying in vain to visualize the facade of the old building. For a few seconds, he even forgot the name of the restaurant.

At the height of his disorientation, he hailed a taxi. The driver explained that the restaurant had moved to a new location some time back, and showed him the skyscraper that now occupied the old address. My father at once remembered everything. *Of course, that was it!* He even recalled having gone to the new location more than once.

When he finally arrived, his friends were finishing their

dessert. They teased him, pretending to believe his excuses. They drank their coffee, paid the bill, and embraced him as they said good-bye. And my father had lunched alone, convinced the waiter was watching him.

I tried to calm him down. Stretching it a bit, I told him that this sort of thing often happened to me. I cited some examples, which didn't seem to impress him: the social occasion I attended wearing shoes that didn't match; the car keys, twice locked inside the car. It was no good; he was still upset.

But at the end of the conversation, his voice grew cheerful. "At least there was one good thing. After dessert, the waiter gave me back my suitcase."

Taking advantage of my silence, he mentioned he had an appointment, and hung up. A few minutes later, I dialed his number. Marta answered.

Speaking softly, she said she was about to call me. The suitcase had indeed reappeared. But none of the clothes belonged to my father except for one shirt—stained with blood.

I asked her not to touch anything, but it was too late; she had already washed the shirt. She was quite nervous, from what I could gather. Her voice on the line trembled.

"What happened to him?"

"Nothing. He probably cut himself shaving. How about the other clothes?"

"I hung them in the office closet."

Embarrassed to the limit, she added, "They're women's clothes."

I sent my assistants home, locked the door, and drank a double scotch, watching the shadows invade the empty rooms around me. Then, lost in the anonymity of a good hour's worth of heavy traffic, I slowly made my way to Laranjeiras.

A single lamp illuminated the living room, its curtains still closed. My father, wearing a white bathrobe, was reading. Seeing me standing there, he didn't look surprised. He removed his glasses and, with his usual affection, held out his arms to me.

Finding him so well disposed, so far removed from the doubts that were assailing me, I decided to confront the subject head-on. After giving him a hug, I sat down on the sofa and asked him about the suitcase. Whose clothes were they? What had happened to the shirt, and where did the bloodstains come from?

He leaned back against the cushions. None of my questions appeared to disturb him in the least. He let out a long sigh and stroked the cover of the volume on his lap. Then he gave me a distant smile, as if he had suddenly moved away in time and space to find refuge in the depths of a labyrinth I would never enter—except through his benevolence.

Reacting to a movement of mine (of impatience, which he interpreted as curiosity), he passed me the book he had been reading moments before. I was going to put it aside, when I saw, to my amazement, that it was written in Arabic.

The book weighed heavily in my hands. The edition was beautiful, bound in real leather, its paper the texture of parchment. It was about three hundred pages long, from what I could judge, divided into eight or ten chapters. The fine print ran loose under my fingers, with the abstract elegance of an enigma.

"How do you like it?" I asked.

"I haven't finished it yet," he replied.

After a brief pause, he added, "So far, I am enjoying it very much."

Besides Portuguese, my father speaks and writes fluent French, a language he learned in his childhood and perfected over the years. He has a reasonable command of English and

Spanish. But that he could have studied Arabic in secret was inconceivable.

I asked if he would read me a passage. With visible pleasure, he accepted. Taking the book from me, he put his glasses on again.

He read two long paragraphs aloud—I believe from the first chapter. The melodic assurance of his voice left no doubts as to the intimacy between reader and text. More than once he smiled to himself, and twice looked at me in a conspiratorial way. When he finished, he closed the volume. He seemed much moved.

"I'll lend it to you when I'm done with it," he promised.

"But I don't know Arabic," I blurted out.

"Neither do I," he replied.

I imagined he might then reveal the language in which the work was written—such was the naturalness with which he spoke. His tone, however, had actually meant *It doesn't really matter.*

For a few minutes we sat in absolute silence, the echo of those words enunciated in an impenetrable language still suspended between us. Marta crossed the room, bearing the coffee tray, which she left on the small table on the terrace. At that point I changed subjects; in my anxiety, I couldn't find a way to unravel a mystery—the full dimensions of which I could not explore without the help of a specialist.

When I got home, I called our family doctor, hoping to get the name of a psychiatrist he could recommend. I told him the story of the suitcase, and mentioned the clothes. But I left out the detail of the bloodstained shirt.

I had barely hung up when the phone rang again. It was Marta, whom I had asked to sleep in the office, so my father couldn't leave the apartment in the middle of the night without her knowing. She had inspected the clothes in the closet more carefully.

"Those clothes . . ." she murmured.

"Yes?"

"They're your mother's. It took me a while to recognize them. But they're hers."

My mother's . . . Where had they come from?

"In the pocket of one of the skirts, there's a letter."

"A letter?"

"Typewritten. No signature."

A letter from my mother . . . or to *my mother?*

At the time of her death, the few jewels she possessed had been given to my sister; her clothes and shoes had been sent to some aunts of mine. But that had all been years ago. . . .

"The skirts and dresses seem to be in good condition. But not the blouses; one of them is torn."

The next morning, I went to the psychiatrist's office. I was received by an affable middle-aged man, who heard me out in silence, taking notes. When I spoke of the book, however, his eyes lit up.

"Fascinating . . ."

We planned for him to visit my father that very afternoon. He instructed me to get hold of the book in the meantime, so we could photocopy the title and the first few pages.

My father usually takes a long nap after lunch. When I left the psychiatrist's office, I phoned Marta. I told her where to look for the book and asked her to take it and the letter she had found downstairs at two o'clock sharp.

"The letter has disappeared."

"Disappeared? How?"

"Your father must have taken it. It looks like he went through your mother's clothes."

At work, I dealt with only some urgent matters. I delegated jobs, canceled meetings, and left early to avoid any problems with traffic. Instead of having lunch at home, I went directly to Laranjeiras, where I ate a sandwich at a bar.

A little before two o'clock, I parked in front of my father's apartment building and waited. A few minutes later, a car stopped behind me. In the rearview mirror I could see the car's two occupants. Both were wearing suits. One of them stayed in the car and the other got out, a small notebook in his hand. He checked the address and walked toward my father's building. Like a sleepwalker, I followed him.

In the entrance hall, the unknown visitor spoke with the doorman. The latter, seeing me arrive, greeted me. "Good afternoon, Mr. Peixoto."

The man turned instantly to me. "Mr. Peixoto?" he asked.

"Yes," I replied without batting an eye.

The doorman was about to clarify the situation, when the elevator door opened. Marta appeared with the book.

"Can you please come with me, sir?" asked the man politely, flashing his badge.

"With pleasure," I said, taking the package from Marta and giving my car keys to the doorman. "Any problem?" I then asked.

"Just a matter we'd like to clear up."

The doorman stood there with his mouth open. My hand firmly on his shoulder, I instructed him in a casual tone. "The car's parked out front. Put it in the garage for me. Or I'll get a ticket. . . ."

From the sidewalk, I called to Marta, who was getting back into the elevator.

"I'll be right back. If the doctor gets here before I do, ask him to wait in the parlor. And offer him some coffee."

"What doctor?" I heard her yell back.

But she was smart; she would figure it out. If not, too bad. The important thing was to get the police out of the way. First and foremost, I needed to find out what the hell they wanted from my father.

I was instructed to sit in the backseat of the car. As soon as we started, I demanded some answers. Under the circumstances, I thought it useful to demonstrate a certain degree of annoyance, a calculated mix of surprise and indignation.

The driver, who was chewing a matchstick with great fondness, said nothing. His companion only replied, without his earlier politeness, that the chief wanted to speak to me. When I persisted, he added, "You've been named as a witness."

"Witness? Of what?"

He turned around and looked at me, examining me carefully for the first time.

"I don't know. All I know is that they want to talk to you."

"And what if you hadn't found me?"

"We would have left written notification."

"Can I read it, then?"

There was an exchange of glances in the front seat. The matchstick rose and fell. The policeman handed me a document. It was a formal summons, and referred only to "a case in progress."

I gave it back and began to leaf through my father's book. The cool breeze gave life to the pages as they passed between my fingers. The words must sound beautiful, I thought, inspired by the abstract letters that rose and fell gracefully like waves, without interruption. Until, as I turned a page, a loose piece of paper materialized in my hands.

The letter, I realized at once.

My father had hidden it in his book. . . . The thin piece of paper, folded in half, was full of small round holes, corresponding to letters that for some reason had suffered from the force of the typewriter keys. Possibly for bearing the brunt of someone's rage when the text was typed.

As Marta had said, there was no signature. Neither was there a date or a recipient's name. The letter started in a particularly abrupt way.

Yesterday at Margarida's party, you raised your skirt for a few seconds so Julia could see your left thigh. The red marks on your skin could have been painted—with enamel or lipstick—but it wouldn't surprise me if they had resulted from scratches clawed in blood.

I raised my head and took a deep breath, my eyes fixed on my companions' necks. I kept on reading, more breathless than ever.

Shameless, to exhibit to a friend the marks of this sickness of yours—because I'm convinced we are dealing here with some sort of perversion.

The braking of the car as we reached the police station interrupted my reading. Still stunned, I placed the letter back inside the book and smiled faintly at the policeman who opened the door. *What madness is this?* I thought, hesitating on the sidewalk.

I was directed to a small waiting room. After inviting me to sit down on a bench, the policeman turned his back and disappeared down the corridor. It was up to the driver—who, still chewing on his matchstick, had followed us in—to keep me company.

I waited for what seemed a very long time—half an hour maybe. Even so, I couldn't bring myself to take another look at the letter, the initial phrases of which continued to torment my mind. It was the language, more than the scene described, that shocked me. I could hardly imagine my father resorting to such intense imagery to express emotions that seemed to have been borrowed from a tabloid. No, the letter could only have belonged to some third party, and found its way into my mother's skirt pocket by accident.

However, there was a problem. Serious enough to connect my parents to the text: My godmother's name was Julia. She had died along with my mother—victim of the same car accident—almost fifteen years ago. An accident from which my father had miraculously escaped unharmed. This was the memory that now turned my insides out.

Finally, the door opened. Several people emerged from the room. In all probability, some sort of meeting had been going on. The police chief appeared in the doorway. With a tired gesture, he waved me in. He was tall and heavy, without coat or tie, and the top of his shirt was unbuttoned. He nodded toward a chair. As he sat down behind his desk with a leisure that struck me as studied, he didn't take his eyes from the book on my lap.

"ID," he said in a dry tone as he picked up the phone and dialed a number.

Surprised, I handed him my papers. Someone must have answered at the other end; the chief said, "He didn't come. But he sent the book. With his son, or some relative. The last name's the same." Then, addressing me, he said with a firm gesture, "Give it here."

The order admitted no refusal. I handed him the heavy volume, which he placed on the table and examined, holding the receiver between his shoulder and ear.

"Right, there's no doubt. It's the one. What now?"

The other fellow said something. The chief looked at me, as if to size me up.

"No, there's no danger of that. He'll never figure it out."

Holding his hand over the mouthpiece, he asked, "Are you his son?"

"Yes."

"Is he going to give up? Or does he want to insist on this?"

My vacant expression could have suggested firmness rather than bewilderment. Keeping his hand over the phone, the man proceeded. "If he gives up, we'll drop the whole thing. Never bring it up again. I'm authorized to make that proposal."

"And the book . . ."

"Forget the book."

He noted the drops of sweat on my forehead.

"I'll call you back in a minute," he said on the phone.

He hung up the receiver and laced his fingers together, cracking all his knuckles at once. Lighting a cigarette, he tilted back his chair and propped his feet up on the desk. Then, nearly causing me to fall off my chair in fright, he bellowed, "MARIO! COFFEE!"

The letter, about to disappear with the book . . . I could still rescue it, of course. But wouldn't it be better to let it go?

I closed my eyes for a few seconds and pictured myself being led through the contours of a minefield. Two stories were tangled together in front of me. Where did one start and the other end? Through what diabolic caprice had they been twined into one single mystery?

"Could you possibly . . ." I began, opening my eyes. I felt my mouth and throat go dry. A wrong question could well mean kissing my past good-bye.

The police chief took a long drag on his cigarette, elbows on the desk, a question taking shape from behind the wrinkles in his forehead.

"Look," he said at last, blowing out an enormous amount of smoke, "either you know all about this"—a new drag on the cigarette, and he completed his thought—"or you're lucky enough not to."

The conclusion, frankly didactic, followed at once.

"If you don't know anything, don't ask. In the circumstances, our offer is reasonable. Take my word for it: Accept it. And we'll drop the whole thing."

The whole thing . . . The key thrown into the depths of the ocean, condemning me, forever, to live immersed in doubts. A key I was throwing away myself.

But was there any real alternative?

"Very well," I replied, turning my eyes toward the fan blades on the ceiling, as the book disappeared into his desk drawer, taking two secrets with it.

As I inhaled deeply, the police chief dialed a number.

"It's a done deal," he said into the receiver without pleasure or pride. Just another duty carried out. The boy with the coffee tray slammed the door open. I stood up with some difficulty and said, "If you'll pardon me, I don't care for coffee."

The police chief gestured amenably: No problem. He gave me back my papers and shook my hand in silence. I left.

In the sunny street, vendors were noisily dismantling their fruit and vegetable stands from the neighborhood's open market. A light odor of spoiled fruit and rotten fish hovered in the air. *Remains from the fair . . .* I thought. A taxi pulled up beside me.

When I got back to Laranjeiras, I found my father in an excited conversation with the psychiatrist. Their enthusiasm was mutual; they hardly acknowledged my greetings. I took advantage of this to relax a bit, and sat listening to them, contributing occasionally with a comment but avoiding my father's eyes.

He didn't come. . . . He sent the book. . . .

Marta, faithful to old habits, took the coffee tray toward the terrace. Outside, the sun was setting, celebrated by the singing of birds and the intermittent honking of cars. As we walked toward the balcony, my father, suddenly intrigued, stopped short, as if he had remembered something. He placed his hand on my arm, briefly locking his eyes on mine.

What was he searching for? And in what worlds, scales, or dimensions? In which of his stories had he lost himself now?

Without hesitation, I offered him what he needed most: my full support. Tacit, serene, unconditional. Regarding the subject that united us at that precise moment: ridding ourselves of the psychiatrist, just as we were rid of the book. Placing the utmost distance between his questions and our answers.

There would always be time, later, to consign pending matters to oblivion.

Albatross

The letter, on top-quality paper bearing a letterhead, came from a notary public in a small rural town. The name of the town meant nothing to him. The contents of the letter, however, were so unexpected that he caught himself groping through the air behind him in search of a chair.

An island . . . He had inherited an island. . . . He who owned nothing more than a few books and prints—and whose rent had been overdue since January. But there was no doubt; the text was clear: ". . . approximately 1.7 square miles, including the woods and beaches contained therein, situated seventeen miles from the coast of . . ."

He telephoned the notary public and confirmed the news with the head officer, a soft-spoken lawyer. His great-uncle, the source of this miracle, a relative he hadn't even heard from in twenty years, had died a few weeks before.

A small island . . . Would it have electricity and safe drinking water?

Inheriting an island at age fifty produces peculiar fantasies in the mind of a man without ambitions. He actually dreamed there might be a treasure chest buried under palm trees. And he was reminded of his childhood, when the greatest joys were always preceded by a certain uneasiness.

The legal formalities took about a month. When the day arrived, he went by bus to a village on the coast. The owner of a banana boat, after carefully inspecting his map, introduced him to a fisherman, who, in exchange for a modest sum, agreed to detour his normal route along the coast and take him to his domain.

His domain . . .

They left that same afternoon. In spite of the ocean's calmness, the boat rocked a little. Low clouds covered the coastline, and islands went by one after another: bigger, smaller, inhabited, apparently deserted, sometimes no more than a pair of rocks. A light drizzle began to fall.

After two hours, the fisherman came over and pointed to a greenish spot on the horizon. He felt an unexpected surge of tenderness for that parcel of the universe, the destiny of which the gods had so casually deposited in his hands.

Was it really deserted, as the lawyer had said? Judging from his conversation during the trip, the fishermen didn't frequent these parts. They preferred the open sea, or trawling along the coast. At most, they had glimpsed an occasional sailboat anchored in the island's cove to shelter overnight.

In another half hour, they arrived. The island was much larger than he had imagined, though two small hills kept him from evaluating its size accurately. It would take a whole day, at least, just to explore it.

He was taken to the beach in a rowboat. It was agreed that he would be picked up in three days, a length of time that suddenly seemed a little excessive. But the quiet elegance of the bay, contrasting with a wild and varied abundance of vegetation, and the warm breeze that had replaced the drizzling rain completely eliminated any doubts he might have had about this adventure.

Because really, that's what it was. An adventure . . . with roots in childhood and a random flavor. Except for the cold, gritty sand under his bare feet, everything in this story seemed unreal.

Besides a small tent and a lantern, he had brought two canvas bags. In the first were food, three bottles of drinking water, two of wine, towels, a blanket. In the second, clothes, a few books, notebooks, pens, a pair of binoculars, and the manuscript of his latest short story.

Once his things were unloaded, he said good-bye to the boatman. For an instant he again hesitated. Nothing remotely akin to fear: a sense of vulnerability, if anything, in the face of the unknown. For the first time in his life, he found himself truly isolated—in a place from which he couldn't return on his own.

But the birds began to sing so cheerfully that he felt welcomed. He breathed deeply and looked with confidence at the man who was rowing back to the fishing boat. A little later, the throttle of the engine, dry and measured, fell on his ears. They waved to each other.

"Don't forget me!" he yelled.

Had the fisherman heard? The boat disappeared around the curve of the island, leaving behind a small plume of black smoke, which soon faded, as well.

He pitched his tent in an elevated spot covered with grass, between the beach and the thick woods. He wanted to get settled before nightfall, which was approaching fast. This spot, he thought, would be ideal for building a house, if he ever had the means. He collected some kindling to build a fire. The damp wood resisted his efforts, so he lit the lantern and set it on a rock. Leaning against a tree trunk, he opened his manuscript.

The page was spattered with blood. Surprised, he glanced up, as if the red droplets might have fallen out of the sky. Then he realized he had cut his finger; there was blood on his shirt and trousers. Licking his wound, he glanced about him and saw the kindling lying on the sand. That was it, he decided, a thorn.

The blood had stained the last two sentences of his text: *The only freedom left to him consisted in frequenting his wife's nightmares. At night, under the sheets, she tossed among the ghosts of imaginary infidelities—and he must appease her jealousy when she awoke.*

He reread the passage, under the asphyxiating spell that had marked the end of his marriage. He closed the notebook and walked down to the beach, wetting his feet in the white foam. The coolness of the water encouraged him. Taking off his clothes, he plunged into the sea.

With a few strokes he was beyond the waves, floating. The cold, however, forced him to go on swimming. Not wanting to stray too far, he veered toward the cove.

He was tired when he reached it. With some difficulty he pulled himself up onto a rock. Rubbing his hands over his dripping body, he hopped up and down on the wet surface. He intended to return as soon as he got his wind back.

In the distance, the flickering light of his lantern sprinkled gold flecks on his tent. The prospect of a dry towel appealed to him. He considered going back on foot, over the rocks, but they were moss-covered and slippery.

Just as he was about to dive back into the water, he heard a sound from far away. Instinctively, he crouched. A breath of air and, again, the sound. A melody . . . carried by the breeze, coming closer and closer. Suddenly, the music stopped. And on his left, almost at his side, a large white sailboat appeared, crossing the space directly in front of him.

Three masts cutting the silence, their sails flapping against the wind with a half-ghostly elegance. *A phantom ship* . . . But at once he distinguished a figure maneuvering the craft from the stern. Beside the central mast was another silhouette. That of a woman, he noticed when she moved.

On the beach, the wind had put out the lantern, plunging his campsite into shadows. The darkness reduced him to an intruder, a feeling his nudity intensified. The couple had by now dropped anchor and fastened the sails.

He left his rock, entering the water without a sound. He swam back to the beach, plagued by doubts. Not that the couple threatened him; on the contrary, the sailboat signaled well-being and security. But it was impossible not to associate its arrival—coming, as it had, on the very heels of his own—with an invasion.

His teeth chattering, he gathered his clothes up from the sand and went into the tent. Vigorously, he rubbed himself dry with the towel. As he dressed, he heard the clinking of dishes, silverware, and glasses in the distance, then a bucket of water being thrown into the sea.

By the time he left the tent, the music had started up again. A baroque piece—Vivaldi, possibly. A table was being set up on the stern as the couple prepared for dinner. Anchored about fifty yards from the beach, the sailboat offered itself up for his inspection. He remembered his binoculars.

Yet, for a moment, he remained motionless. Except for the intriguing coincidence of this meeting, nothing had occurred on either side, up to that point, that would suggest real intrusion. But if he gave in to the temptation to spy on the couple, the precarious balance would be broken. Better to sleep. With any luck, the sailboat would be on its way by morning.

He considered facing his manuscript again. Could the blood have injected new life into his words? Impossible to know without lighting the lantern. His resistance weakened second by second. A desire—intense, secret, dangerous—contaminated him with an almost youthful energy. He found himself rummaging feverishly through his bags. That intimacy, soon to be violated, would become his treasure.

He looked through the binoculars; the tips of the masts appeared in his lenses. Slowly he lowered his angle, adjusting the focus. As his field of vision descended, the light filled it with details of every sort. He passed over them all without pausing. Above all, it was the couple he wanted to see. At the bottom of the mast he stopped, his heart pounding fast.

The music seemed to be louder now. Or was it an illusion, induced by the closeness of his lenses? The refined melody dominated the air with the clarity of a live performance. The woman had disappeared inside the cabin. On the bridge, the man was calmly opening a bottle of wine.

He, too, calmed himself. Time was his ally. Better yet, his accomplice. He turned the binoculars toward the bow, trying in vain to read the boat's name. The woman was coming back; immediately, he focused on her.

He was surprised she had dressed so formally for dinner. She wore a pearl necklace, a white tunic that swept down to her sandals, and a turquoise-blue stole, which slid off one shoulder. Her casual, almost careless gestures as she approved the wine, one hand on her waist, the other holding a glass up in the air, suggested complete affinity with a world of sophistication and refinement.

They sat on opposite sides of the table, both in profile to

him, the woman to the right, the man to the left. The slight elevation from which he watched permitted him a privileged view. Wrapping himself in a blanket against the cold, he once again leaned against the tree.

He studied the woman first. She was young, barely thirty. Blond, slender, with a short hairdo. More than the freshness of her youth, he envied the shower she had just taken. The sailboat undoubtedly possessed generous facilities with plenty of fresh hot water, the only luxury he missed so far—his skin, saturated with salt, chafed under his shirt. He imagined her to be lightly perfumed. The man, in his forties, was tall and stout. His tanned skin suggested a healthy outdoor lifestyle, which the very dimensions of the sailboat seemed somehow to confirm. In shorts and a T-shirt, he savored the wine, tilting his head back toward the sky.

Suddenly hungry, he remembered the chicken sandwich he had prepared for his first night. He took it out of its wrapper, embellished it with two leaves of lettuce, and opened a bottle of wine, raising a toast to his visitors' health.

The three of them dined, united by the melody. From time to time, he consulted his binoculars. At one point he heard them laughing. He felt an enormous desire to get closer to them, the way a stranger in a tavern draws near the fireplace, rubbing his hands together. If it weren't for the cold and his fear of being discovered, he would have swum over to the sailboat, just to listen to them.

It was then he noticed something. Something so unnerving that he lowered the binoculars, as though needing to confirm with his naked eyes what the lenses showed: a pistol.

It was under the table, on the woman's lap. A silver-handled pistol, half hidden under her napkin. He focused on the man. He was laughing happily.

Jumping to his feet, he upset his glass of wine. He took a few steps forward. On the deck of the sailboat, the man had also risen, and was going down toward the cabin.

Alone at the table, the woman lit a cigarette. She turned her eyes toward the island. It was improbable that she could distinguish the beach or the forest in any detail. Nevertheless, his hands tightened on the binoculars, as if her gaze could pierce him.

My God, he thought, his breath short. She was going to shoot. Any minute now. Those eyes didn't suggest bitterness or ferocity, only determination. Between one remark and another—after dessert, before the liqueur—she would shoot.

The man returned with another bottle of wine, already open. Standing with a napkin draped over his arm, he bowed ceremoniously to his companion, serving her with the rapture of an adolescent. For the second time, she approved the wine.

What if he yelled? If he tore the night with a bloodcurdling scream?

The cold water at his feet brought him up with a start. Without realizing it, he had strayed toward the beach. With the change of angle, however, he could no longer follow the woman's gestures. The music stopped; neither of them seemed disposed to change it. A dangerous silence weighed down the air. His heart was beating out of control. From the bottom of his chest, he heard his voice rising like a wave gathering in the dark.

"VIVALDI!" he yelled.

The woman startled in astonishment. The man, jumping up, bent over the rail. With surprising agility, he ran to the other end of the deck and put out the lights on the sailboat.

"Who's there?" he bellowed.

A strong voice, but hesitant. He said something to the

woman, who went down to the cabin. Again he called out, more irritated than alarmed. "Who's there?"

The woman reappeared, carrying something in her hands. A powerful beam of light flashed across the beach. Waving his arms, he shouted, "Good evening!"

Still waving, he repeated his greeting. "Good evening! Welcome!"

And when the searchlight finally hit him, he called, "I heard music."

Blinking in the harsh glare, he felt the most pathetic of men. Once again he shouted, "Welcome!"

He kept the binoculars behind his back, fastened to his belt. Now it was the couple who examined him, with lenses sure to be powerful. Never did he cease waving or smiling. He added additional information to his speech. "I'm the owner of the island! Make yourselves at home."

The searchlight played over him, scanning the night. A voice echoed, this time lower, almost tired. "What a scare!"

An enormous pause followed.

"We always stop here. We've never seen anyone before. Do you live here?"

"No. I'm just camping. I was over on the other side of the island when you arrived."

He couldn't seem to lower his voice, in spite of the difficulty of maintaining a dialogue at the top of his lungs with any degree of naturalness. He added, "Beautiful sailboat."

The man, relaxing a little, repeated what he had said before. "What a scare."

"I'm sorry."

"No, that's all right. . . . Are you a fisherman? Is this island really yours?"

Instead of answering, he asked, "Was that Vivaldi?"

"What?" the other yelled back, surprised.

"The music. Was it Vivaldi?"

"Corelli," said the woman. And again, louder, "Corelli."

He latched onto the name like a drowning man would a life ring.

"Corelli! Of course, Corelli."

The man cut him off. "Well, good night, then. See you in the morning." The light went out abruptly.

Lost in the darkness, he replied, "Good night."

Sweat was rolling off him in streams and his legs trembled. He thought of the gun. Once more he called, "Hey!"

"What is it?" asked the man almost roughly.

"Your sailboat! What's her name?"

"*Albatross.*"

"*Albatross . . .*"

"Good night!" It was her voice this time.

Had she left the pistol in the cabin when she went down? Or was it still wrapped in the napkin?

"Good night!" he called back.

He sat down on the sand, completely exhausted. A cold breeze blew over him. *I'm leaving, but I'll be back,* Death whispered in his ears. He breathed with difficulty. *I know,* he thought. *I know.*

A night . . . He had gained a night. Maybe a day or two. He crawled back to the tent and relighted the lantern. On the sailboat, two lights came on also, one inside, the other, weaker, on the stern. The music started again: jazz, this time.

Piano, bass, percussion, saxophone . . . He moved around outside the tent, with the express purpose of being seen. Then he strolled toward the trees, as if to urinate. Protected by the vegetation, he took out the binoculars again.

In the kitchen, the man was busy doing the dishes, his body

swaying to the rhythm of the music. Directly above him, the woman was smoking, leaning over the rail as she watched the island.

She could not possibly see him. Even so, he felt he was being observed. For his part, he couldn't discern her features in the shadows, only the lighted point of the cigarette and the outline of her figure, arms crossed.

Vivaldi . . . she must have been thinking.

Vivaldi . . . A single despairing cry had landed him in the tangled center of someone else's labyrinth. The man hadn't even noticed. How could he, if he didn't know what was at stake?

But the woman suspected something. And there she stood, smoking, watching him, wondering. Somewhere in the firmament, Death drummed its fingers impatiently on a barroom countertop. It would be back, surely. But when?

Unless . . .

He felt assailed by a strange force. Back at the tent, fully illuminated by the lantern, he deliberately fixed the binoculars on the woman.

She moved back two steps and looked in all directions, as if a thousand demons were spying on her.

In the kitchen, the man was now drying his dishes in sync with the music. At the bow, the woman threw her cigarette into the sea, as though she had come to a decision, and strode quickly toward the rear of the boat. Was she going to denounce him?

When she reached the stairway, however, she stopped and came back to the rail. Placing both hands on the varnished wood, she stayed there directly in his line of vision, as though to defy him.

He lowered the binoculars and turned his gaze away, overtaken by a weariness bordering on disgust. There was nothing to be done. Now it was only a question of time.

Seeing his glass overturned on the ground, he refilled it with wine. He lifted it in a toast to the sea without looking at the sailboat. *Have a great trip,* he thought. *Kill each other, devour each other . . .*

But somewhere else, far away . . . He hadn't landed in his new domain that precise afternoon for nothing. The gods hadn't entrusted the destiny of that island to him by chance. Discounting the few drops that had fallen on his manuscript, blood wouldn't be spilled here.

After a few more minutes, he raised his eyes to the boat again. The music had now stopped for good. The woman, her back to the island, was completely still.

Something in her attitude had changed. Something almost imperceptible. He grabbed the binoculars. Her body had lost its rigidity. Head down, she seemed to be sobbing.

He put out the lantern, leaving the couple alone. So they could tally up the scores, without violating the natural order of things. It was asking too much, he knew.

Just before sleep overtook him, however, he heard the music begin again, and he identified the piece. This time there was no doubt: Vivaldi. He slept.

The next morning when he woke up, the *Albatross* had left.

The three days following those first hours spent on the island passed slowly. No matter how rich the vegetation around him, or how varied the number of butterflies and birds flying overhead, he thought only of the woman. Not even the discovery of a tiny coral beach surrounded by palm trees, directly across the island from his hills, could distract him from his obsession.

His memories of her blended into the perfume of the sea breeze and the shades of the evening colors, insinuating themselves into every fold of his imagination. What was her relationship to the man? Was she a wife, lover, friend, sister?

We always stop here. We've never seen anyone before.

The remark suggested a degree of familiarity with the region. She had obviously participated in other sailing trips at various times, possibly happy ones. What was she doing now as she skirted an abyss?

The abyss had been hers; the vertigo was now his. Would she honor the terms of her promise? Suggestion, really, more than promise. Validated, at most, by a few measures of music.

He spent a good part of the second night sitting on the grassy hill, his eyes on the sea. The third night found him swimming toward the cove in the dark.

Over and over he recalled the first glance she had given the island—the glance he had immediately captured in his lenses. As time passed, he retrieved from the depths of those pupils a dimension of sadness that had at first eluded him.

Had it really been there?

The doubt, uncomfortable and relentless, began to occupy an ever-greater space in his thoughts. Had the episode originated from a coolly designed plan, motivated by greed? Or had the whole drama been rooted in fear or despair?

He spent his nights revisiting every word of the conversation they had had.

"Vivaldi!"

He saw the silhouette jumping up from the chair, the man's shadow sliding toward the stern, the beam of light slicing the darkness.

"Who's there?"

Each of them had played a different instrument in an improvised score. He had shouted firm notes imbued with certainty, which reverberated like those of a trumpet. The man had deflected each one, as if they had been dull bullets ricocheting from his cymbals. Until the woman had brought harmony to the scene: "*Corelli.*"

In that baroque mirror they had found each other. From that point on, they would proceed together, on the same score, she vulnerable in her waiting, he powerless in the dark.

"*Corelli! Of course.*"

His decision to search for the woman matured gradually, as he came to feel responsible for her destiny. Without defining precisely what form this affair might assume, he counted the hours left until the fisherman's return.

They finally passed. And the little fishing boat came back, preceded by the syncopated drumming of its engine. He said good-bye to the island.

On the return trip, he felt he was being observed. Was it his imagination? Maybe . . . In any case, the fisherman respected his silence, limiting his remarks to comments about the weather and the duration of the crossing.

It was raining when they got to the village. He walked on the wet cobblestones toward the bus stop. His bus wouldn't be coming for a while, so he went into a bar and ordered a cup of hot coffee, which he savored as he planned his next moves.

"*We always stop here. . . .*"

The adverb implied they had not come from too far away. He would concentrate his search—at least initially—within a radius of one hundred miles along the shoreline, to the north and south of the island. Unclear as to the probable outcome of his investigation, he wavered between a boyish excitement and a sense of anguish—the contours of which he preferred to leave undefined.

At home he took a long shower and fell into bed, exhausted.

He dreamed about his island, and woke with the sails of the *Albatross* beating the wind amid the curtains of his window.

The inquiries he made during the next two weekends produced no results. No one had heard of the sailboat in the places he visited. It didn't matter; in a way, he actually preferred to postpone a discovery, the consequences of which he still had no way of ascertaining. In spite of the long bus trips over potholed roads, he sighed with relief at every dead end. And he wrote avidly, as if the deeper background of that episode had fertilized his ideas.

But as time went on, he started to get impatient. He even began to cultivate the illusion that the *Albatross* was avoiding him. This sensation grew even sharper on his third trip, when a boy promised to take him to the boat—and led him instead to a plain fishing vessel beached on a sandbank.

He finally paid a visit to the port authorities—an alternative that, till then, he had chosen to avoid. It bothered him that dusty old registry books might facilitate a reencounter he would have preferred, as much as possible, to leave to chance.

He discovered two vessels registered under that same name, both in private marinas situated between ports he had visited. The first was a yacht, the second a sailboat.

The following weekend, he rented a car. The day was bright, and there was little traffic on the roads. He arrived at his destination within three hours. At a gas station, the attendant pointed out the side road that would take him to the property.

The narrow road descended toward the shore. After driving a short distance, he left the car hidden among the trees and walked to the edge of a cliff. In a small bay, moored at a pier, stood the *Albatross*.

It was the same sailboat, without a doubt. So still, however, it looked more like a domesticated animal. Its sails rolled up under canvas covers and fastened to the masts, its hull against the wooden pier, the *Albatross* now seemed part of a setting that included the ocean and the thick woods beyond. The sailboat shared the stage with a colonial-style house and a beach of reddish sand—both deserted.

The house, one story tall, was surrounded by an ample lawn. Its ivy-covered roof projected out over a veranda. Five blue window frames were outlined on the white facade, and closed venetian blinds highlighted the loneliness of the sailboat in the morning sun.

Suddenly, very close, he heard children laughing, and immediately afterward the barking of a dog. He walked a little way through the trees. Almost at his feet, a second house appeared. It was much smaller, rustic, and a circle of banana trees grew around it. In the bare yard of beaten earth, half a dozen chickens pecked at the ground. A little girl ran outside, followed by a smaller boy. Laughing, they scampered up the hillside, the dog bounding after them. When they saw him, they came to an abrupt halt. The dog began to bark furiously. A woman appeared in the yard, wiping her hands on a dishcloth.

"Good afternoon!" he called.

"Good afternoon," replied the woman.

The dog stopped barking. A silence loaded with curiosity fell on the scene. Before their surprise could turn to suspicion, he gestured vaguely in the direction of the road.

"My car broke down," he said quite naturally. "Is there a telephone around here?"

As he spoke, he went down the path, the children backing away, the dog growling. He asked the girl playfully, "Does he bite?"

The woman was sorry, but there was no telephone here.

The closest one was back at the gas station. Right along the main road, about a mile away.

He sat down on a rock and shook his head, feigning good-humored discouragement. *A mile!* He sensed that his city clothes imposed respect, and that his graying hair would inspire confidence. He patted the dog.

"It's not so far, really," said the little girl, trying to cheer him up.

"And there's a mechanic there," added her brother.

Smiling at both of them, he commented, "I saw a house from the road up there . . . and a sailboat."

"In the boss's house, there's a phone," the little girl said, interrupting, "but we can't use it."

"It's out of order," the mother added quickly.

"That's all right," he reassured her. "It doesn't matter. I'll walk to the gas station."

For a few seconds, he looked at the shabby house. The woman was watching him closely, the children beside her.

"Nice-looking boat," he commented in a conversational tone.

"It's sailed all around the world!" exclaimed the boy.

"They're selling it," said the girl excitedly.

"Selling it?" He couldn't disguise his shock. For the first time, his voice sounded real. The details all around him came into sharper focus.

"Yes, it's for sale," confirmed the mother.

"Then I'll buy it!" he joked.

The woman giggled, hiding her wrinkles in the dishcloth. The dog wagged its tail, pleased with the children's happiness.

"It must be very expensive," he went on, more at ease.

"Millions!" cried the boy, stretching his arms wide into the sky.

"But why sell such a beautiful boat?"

Here mother and children exchanged awkward glances.

"It's 'cause the lady died," the boy said, scuffing the ground with his foot.

"The boss is very sad." The girl sighed.

"He may even sell the house," added the woman resignedly.

Their sadness turned to apprehension as his shadow suddenly swayed menacingly over them.

"Are you all right, sir?"

The boy huddled close to the mother. The girl clapped her hand to her mouth, as though stifling a cry.

"It's just the heat," he managed to mumble as he sank down on the rock again.

The woman went into the house and came back with a glass of water.

"Died? But how?" he asked with such a feeble voice, he could barely listen himself.

"Drowned, poor thing."

Still pale, he drank the water.

"She was very nice. She liked the children."

"She gave me a doll," the girl said. "Want to see it?"

He smiled at the woman as the girl ran inside the house. She smiled back, full of sympathy for his shock.

The little girl came back, bringing the doll, accompanied by her brother, who carried a toy car. The four of them sat there in the yard examining these treasures. Little by little, he distanced himself from the desire to know more. He only wanted to sit there, lost in the contemplation of the toys. Above all, he wanted to forget. He had been part of a story—which had changed course. And from which he now felt excluded.

Perhaps for that very reason, the facts came to him in a natural and calm manner, as though his silence generated a vacuum that sucked in all the details and regrouped them at his feet. Pieces of information emerged delicately, none of them requiring any immediate reaction on his part.

The woman had slipped on the wet quarterdeck and fallen from the sailboat in the middle of the night, three weeks ago. A few days later, her body had washed up on the beach not far away. "Her face was all eaten by the fish," the boy added, taking advantage of a pause.

They spoke slowly, in soft voices, each solemnly bringing back a fragment of the past. The words hurt him—he had no way of assimilating them. He thought about the woman, whose flesh by now was rotting beneath the earth.

"We heard about it from the boss. That same night. He came to get the spare key to the house, you see. My husband gave it to him."

"He was shaking from head to toe."

"They found the other key in her pocket."

In panic, the man had radioed for help from the sailboat when he realized she was missing. Various boats had spent hours combing the waters in vain, over a radius of several miles.

"She wasn't a good swimmer."

"She drowned fast. It was very dark."

That was true. On that night, he remembered well, he had spent hours sitting on the grass, gazing into the darkness, redrawing the silhouette of the woman on the *Albatross*. Meanwhile . . .

"He cried so hard!"

The mother bent over her son.

"Cried?" she asked, puzzled.

"First he talked on the phone. Then he cried. He banged his head on the table."

The boy hadn't been able to sleep. He had crept outside,

gone down the path to the big house, and peeked through a window. Now he confessed his mischief.

"And he didn't see you?"

"He was drunk."

The man had guzzled two bottles and then passed out, slumping onto the table. The boy had only left the window in the wee hours of the morning, when the police arrived.

The inquiry confirmed the accident. The woman had been buried in the city.

"My husband went. There were lots of people. Lots of flowers."

Three weeks ... So it had all happened on the trip back from the island. Three weeks ...

She must have changed her mind. She must have tried to kill her husband.

Only she had hesitated. A struggle, a bullet that missed the mark—and she had fallen overboard. Or had she been thrown into the water?

Had she screamed?

The boat had sailed away, disappearing in the night.

Worse, it had stayed just out of her reach, sails furled, rocking in the water.

So many hypotheses ... and they all made sense. Except that none of them sounded real. They paled before the emptiness that overwhelmed him.

He had no reason to judge the husband, or to incriminate him. Suppose a wave hadn't thrown the woman off balance—then *he* might have disappeared into the sea. With a bullet through his forehead and an anchor tied to his feet. Perhaps that was why he had drunk so much that night, why he had wept in despair.

He considered taking a closer look at the sailboat but

couldn't find the strength to do it. He said good-bye to the woman and children and went up the hill, walking away from the questions he left behind.

Six months went by. When summer came, he began to feel an intense desire to return to the island. This time, he decided, he would stay longer. He wanted to look over the collection of stories that consumed his nights, and catch up on his reading. He might have other reasons for going back to his domain. But he had long ceased thinking about them.

At the small port, the fisherman he knew was having problems with his boat's engine and couldn't take him to the island. But the man introduced him to a friend, who agreed to do the job. The fellow even left him the dinghy he was towing as a bonus, fruit of a spontaneous camaraderie developed during the crossing.

Thanks to the dinghy, he gained mobility. He paddled daily around the island, uncovering all sorts of details from various angles. On his first visit, he had familiarized himself with the physical dimensions of the landscape. Now he had the luxury of courting the island from a distance, discovering its bends and cliffs with renewed enchantment. He spent hours floating in the water, reading, half asleep, his fishing rod propped at his feet.

One day, to protect himself from the sun that had been beating down since early morning, he improvised a tent roof on his small boat. There he stayed, under its canvas, bent over his book, waiting for the fish to bite. From time to time his line would jerk, though nothing much materialized on his hook. Twice he replenished the bait. Till he finally gave it up, he was so absorbed in his reading. After a length of time he couldn't have estimated precisely, he heard, behind him, a dull thumping sound.

A keel beating hard against the water, he thought. He turned around and saw the sailboat. So close—almost on top of him—that it seemed about to cut his dinghy in two. A line of letters, painted on the leaning bow, paraded before his eyes. And the *Albatross,* in a salty cloud, passed within a few inches of him.

He struggled to get up, losing his balance in the waves. The canvas shelter and the oars fell into the ocean. Gripping the seat of the fragile boat, he saw the man waving at him.

So it hadn't been sold. . . . The Albatross hadn't been sold! Lifted by a luminous flash, which in one fell swoop eliminated all and every hint of melancholy from the face of the Earth, it again put his island on the map.

The woman was back. With all the honors bestowed upon her by ghosts from countless seas, she was back for a last sailing trip.

He fished the oars out of the water, collected and folded up his canvas, and returned slowly to the beach. He pulled the dinghy onto the sand, leaving it under the bushes, as was his habit. For a moment, he stood motionless, looking at his hills.

He thought about the man who, on the other side of the island, was busy anchoring his sailboat on the little coral beach. It seemed natural that he should come back. This route was familiar to him. One could even say that there was something predictable about this reencounter. It was the way it had happened that worried him.

They had almost collided. . . . With great dexterity, however, the man had managed to avoid the worst. Steering the sailboat away, he had waved an apology and disappeared around the bend of the cove.

The sequence of events hadn't lasted more than a minute or

so. But it had left in its wake a sensation bordering on uneasiness. As if the episode fulfilled a function that he failed to grasp.

He had a bite to eat, without much appetite, and settled down under the trees, book in hand. Sooner or later, the man would show up.

Hours passed. He had a long swim; the afternoon fell. When the sun went down, he lit a fire. The green wood gave him some trouble, and he blew on the coals for a long while. He was still squatting down, puffing, when the man approached, carrying a bottle of liquor. He had come by way of the trail that twisted among the trees to the right of the hills.

Drawing closer, the visitor nodded with a somewhat studied formality, and produced a remark calculated for effect.

"My respects to the owner of the island."

Owner . . . The greeting, spoken in a jovial tone, transported them offhandedly into the past, and reinstated the woman between them.

"You *are* the owner of the island?" the man insisted good-humoredly.

"Yes, I am," he replied in the same tone.

"I'm sorry I startled you today," the man said, holding out a hand.

Another echo from the past. Wasn't it he who had startled the couple on that remote night?

"It was a bit close," he admitted, shaking the man's hand.

He offered him his folding canvas chair, and went to get some glasses. His feet felt like lead. The man poured them drinks.

"Cheers."

"Cheers"

Brandy . . . Two men drinking brandy on a deserted island.

"An inheritance," he commented vaguely, with a gesture that embraced the island, the ocean, and the stars.

The other didn't react to this explanation. He was examining the tent with interest. Was he thinking about his wife? Had he been witness to, or agent of, her death?

"I still don't really know what to do with it," he went on, aware that he spoke with the express purpose of filling the silence. As if the island were a painting he couldn't decide where to hang, or an old piece of furniture acquired at some third-rate auction. In a last attempt, he added, almost to himself, "It's a shame there's no drinking water."

"Drinking water?" The man turned to face him. "But there is. And lots of it."

The man's tone was attentive, almost solicitous.

"Where?" he asked, surprised.

The other laughed and replied, "In the pirates' cave."

"The pirates' cave?" He laughed, too.

To his surprise, however, the man wasn't joking. Drawing in the sand with a stick, he explained where the place was. The entrance was hidden by vegetation, and in the afternoon the tide rose to cover it. But in the morning it was visible. The springwater came from a pit below the rocks. It was fresh and abundant. Taking another swallow, he added, "It was my wife who discovered it. By accident."

He shuddered at how effortlessly the wife had entered the scene, and wanted to change the subject, out of fear or shame. It was too early for her to take shape between the two of them. But the man continued.

"She was lying on the floating mattress, half asleep. The current took her there."

He seemed determined to bring her into the conversation. He was creating a stage setting for her, rich in suggestive detail, almost forcing the other to visualize her drowsing in the sun, one arm trailing through the water.

What had she been thinking about as she floated on the clear sea? The death of the husband who was now recalling her to life?

He examined the man closely. He wore a scuffed pair of tennis shoes, shorts, and a T-shirt. The man was older than he had imagined a few months ago, when he had framed him in his lenses. He decided they were about the same age.

The man pulled his chair closer to the fire, poured himself another shot, and passed the bottle to his companion. He then asked how he spent his time on the island, and what he did for a living. Learning that he was a writer, the man seemed interested. His gaze, however, remained distant, veiled.

So he told him about the book of short stories he had just finished, knowing full well that his words were being lost in the shadows of the night. As he spoke, he thought about the woman, and how best to bring her back into the conversation.

For a moment, she had allowed herself to appear, exposing her warm, salty skin and graceful body to the universe. Then, as if by magic, she had left the scene again. Now she swayed between fire and breeze, life and death. Waiting.

At some point they would have to face her. But when? The man was gazing at the ocean. There before them, in the space the moon was just beginning to illuminate, they had dined together for the last time. Did he remember in detail what had happened that night?

An unexpected thought flashed through his mind: *The caretaker had talked.*

The caretaker had talked. . . . Alerted by his wife and children, he had mentioned to his boss that a stranger had visited the property. Odd, his interest in the sailboat, the caretaker had probably said. Odder still, the intensity with which he had reacted to the news of the accident involving the boss's wife. And what about the lie regarding the car's breakdown? His kid had followed the stranger all the way to the main road—the car was fine.

Intrigued, the husband had asked around. At the gas station near his property. In the marinas where his boat sometimes docked. He had grown convinced that someone was on his trail. Who could it be? And why?

At first, he must have thought it was the police. Maybe an extra zealous inspector or a private detective. But as the months went by, he had discarded that possibility—and gone further back in time. He had returned to that night on the island when he and his wife had dined on the deck of the *Albatross*. Gradually, sifting through every detail of that night, he had come to the singular cry that had pierced the silence.

The man's eyes were fixed on his. He heard him murmur, "I always did like short stories. . . ."

His words sounded calm enough, conspiratorial, almost sleepy. But they came from far, far away. "Even as a boy I liked to read."

The other woke from his torpor, realizing that they had both been silent for some time. The man was in no hurry. But now he was inviting him to continue.

"Well, I didn't," he replied casually. "I wasn't interested in literature until I was much older."

Night was falling, the bottle almost empty—it was time for the woman to reappear. He decided to escort her through the wings and bring her onstage.

"I started writing through the influence of a girlfriend. Later we married. When she left me, many years later, the passion remained."

"For your stories." The other chuckled.

"For my stories," he confirmed.

And mentally he thanked his ex-wife for coming to his aid. In her honor, he added a specific detail. "Her name was Regina."

"Was?" the other asked.

He hadn't blinked. Nothing seemed to escape his attention. Depending on the role he had played in his wife's death, it was entirely possible he was bent on violence.

The discovery, softened by the brandy, made him dizzy. The feeling was not altogether unpleasant. Could he be drunk? He felt somehow invulnerable. His island had become a huge parchment, where many stories could be written in arabesques of fire. If the man chose to postpone the rituals ordained for that particular night, he would insist the man continue. He would force him to, if necessary. He wasn't afraid of death. Moreover, he had an advantage over him: He had saved his life. Surely the gods couldn't be indifferent to that.

Taking a deep breath, he repeated the verb that still echoed between them. "And your wife, what was her name?"

The words hung suspended in the air. His heart was pounding. He swallowed the rest of his drink in one gulp.

The other, shaking his head pensively, seemed not to have heard. Was he leaning over the ocean once again, watching his wife disappear under the waves?

He stared hard at the man, knowing that he was witnessing a decisive moment in the life of a human being. As he watched, an emotion sprang up from the ground between them, almost palpable. A second theory took shape in his mind, less dramatic, more complex.

Then he understood. And when he saw tears running down the other's face, he was not surprised. The man knew nothing about him. He had come back simply to relive, on the island, the last night he had spent with her. This was the cloak he had chosen for the occasion—this mantle of sadness. Whatever had happened on the sailboat, the man was innocent. The despair the caretaker's son had witnessed, now clearly written all over the wrinkled face, was eloquent proof of that.

"I'm sorry," the other said finally, his trembling hand wiping the tears from his face.

He, too, was deeply moved. So much so that he hardly understood what happened next. The man had drawn a pistol from his pocket.

"I'm sorry," he repeated sadly, as if he deeply regretted what he was about to do.

They stood up slowly, each haunted on opposite sides of the fire. He turned toward the sea, aware that the woman awaited him. An instant before the shot, he heard her voice.

"Corelli . . ."

The bullet hit him. Smiling, he slumped slowly down as the man fired again.

Turn of the River

No one could trace the secret roots of Skinny Pedro's devotion to the world of machines. Yet nobody doubted the young man's earnestness as he read and reread old instruction manuals that kept arriving in the camp on a fairly steady basis, despite the exasperating sluggishness of the banana boats, which wound their way upriver to connect that forgotten part of the jungle to the rest of the world.

Some thought the mystery bore a direct relation to the green tangle that tightly encircled the two dozen shacks balanced precariously between the rain forest and the yellowish waters. Indeed, the diverse lush tones joined forces with the suffocating heat of the jungle to disguise an essential monotony, the primary function of which was to drive crazy anyone who might be inclined to formulate an original thought. Skinny Pedro's obsession might therefore derive from some sort of insanity.

Others were convinced the enigma could be explained in a much simpler, more prosaic way: It had its roots in the river silt, from which no one had extracted gold or any kind of precious stones for months, but the sticky texture of which bespoke a desire to reclaim the immense resources stolen from nature.

Skinny Pedro must certainly have fallen victim to some kind of sorcery.

Whatever the reason, the fact was the young man felt called to a purpose, which he repeated aloud to whoever would listen: The day would come when he would build and fly his own airplane.

An outrageous ambition, given that he was stuck in an outpost whose end had been decreed a few months earlier by the very men who had created and funded it. The act of extinction, formalized thousands of miles away during the course of a tense meeting, had involved opposing factions in the company responsible for the destiny of Skinny Pedro and his companions.

"We can't just leave those people out there, can we?" pondered the employee on whom the future of that handful of men depended.

"For the last six months they've been a dead loss to us. Let them come back on their own if they can!" retorted the manager, brandishing his report, as if the river's refusal to produce any more gold was due to the prospectors' incompetence.

When, many years later, Skinny Pedro had learned the details of this particular meeting, he wasn't surprised. The forest had taught him that city dwellers could often be regulated by cruel and rather unpredictable codes.

Not to mention unfair. God knew how hard they had all worked to fill the quotas fixed by the company, churning through mud that had become the source of a collective hysteria. The prospectors liked to compare the warm, unctuous caress of the silt on their legs and thighs to the kisses of ten thousand lips, rather than imagine that the river had nothing to offer them—except mud.

It had all been in vain. The gold, modest in quantity even in the early days, had simply disappeared. The geological maps had proved useless. Either that or the wrong people had been bribed. The camp was simply crossed off the map. The breeze would spread the sweetish odor of death through the forest and the animals would take care of the rest.

Except for Skinny Pedro, none of the men doubted the company's good intentions. Not even those who, inspired by occasional bouts of yellow fever, had sure access to fleeting moments of lucidity. They all believed that in some large city (the exact location of which remained unknown to them), company managers were actually dedicating their best energies to relocating a labor force that, besides being cheap, had never given them the slightest cause for complaint. Throughout the history of gold panning, workers had never been abandoned in remote or forgotten areas of the jungle. It didn't occur to anyone that it might be expensive to bring back what had cost so little in the first place.

In the beginning, everything went on almost as usual. The jungle quickly swallowed the little landing strip used by the small planes on their weekly visits, but the banana boats continued to resupply the almost sixty men for some time. And even if it had been two months since the last boat had disappeared downriver, with much waving on both sides, there was no reason to worry: Thanks to Skinny Pedro, they wouldn't starve.

For he had been given the task of coordinating the fishermen in charge of feeding the prospectors. A job he had accepted happily, as from his boyhood he had loved to fish—and furthermore, it was no good questioning the foreman's commands. A violent type who never separated himself from the camp's only available gun, the foreman was feared by everyone because of his strength and the nonchalance with which he seemed ready to dispose of other men's lives.

But Skinny Pedro had accepted the task for another, more

important reason. The long hours spent fishing were also good for meditating and reinforced his belief in the destiny marked out for him. He was convinced that the sum of knowledge he had acquired in his boyhood, simple but rich in wisdom, made him a chosen man. A man, above all, in tune with the drama unfolding around him. From long analysis of the intricate diagrams in his manuals—a solitary exercise that provided his reasoning process with an almost alarming clarity—he came to realize that the camp had been abandoned to survive on its own. And since it was unlikely that other banana boats would visit that particular section of the river, which had never been part of their usual routes, he further reasoned that it wouldn't take long for collective despair and violence to fall on the outpost.

Being entrusted with such secret knowledge conferred a special power on Skinny Pedro.

He felt protected by the same serenity that from time immemorial has illuminated the souls of warriors and martyrs. Thus, instead of injecting doubts in his companions' certainties, he read and reread his manuals. Under the noonday sun while fishing, or stealing light from the full moon, the point of his pencil traced the imaginary movements of the washers, threads, coil springs, cylinders, bolts, and screws that had long enriched the workings of his mind. Enthusiastically, he took apart and reassembled the only generator that could still be made to work in the camp—in the unlikely event that a special ball bearing, ordered six months back, materialized among the bananas.

Poking and puttering in this oily domain helped keep his fingers in shape. He had no reason to doubt the invisible links uniting machines of all kinds in a brotherhood accessible to men of his caliber. The lesson learned in his childhood concerning the fluid relationship among fish, plants, birds, and animals must certainly have its equivalent in the no less animated world of engines and machines.

Pedro had no surname; his nickname came from his days at the orphanage. Short in stature, he had long frizzy hair, bright eyes, and hard muscles. Part Indigenous, part Black, he had dark skin that defied the sun; when night came, it let him melt discreetly into the shadows. Then his eyes shone like lamps among the trees. Where he came from, he didn't know; he had simply *arrived* in a boat, as a very small child, like so many others before him. But he had been raised in Acajatuba, a small village on the banks of the Rio Negro.

Adopted son of the forest, he had grown up playing soccer with the natives and the missionaries of a sect for which he still felt deep affection, thanks to the prevailing tolerance of its members. He had learned to read and write from these men in their white robes, who spent most of their time cataloging leaves, roots, and seeds, the latter planted lovingly in little labeled pots that, twice a month, were placed in the backseat of a pickup truck and destined to fly away, by courtesy of two small planes, and disappear mysteriously into the skies over the Amazon.

They didn't do a lot of praying, those monks; and for that reason they were esteemed by the locals. They seemed to be particularly interested in the health of the Indigenous people and recorded in great detail the answers that, between chuckles and puffs on their pipes, the less bashful members of the surrounding tribes gave to their patiently formulated questions. Zealously, they transcribed their own observations on the relationship between certain plants and diseases into notebooks, which they then locked up in a small cupboard.

These missionaries revealed another world to Skinny Pedro on the day they allowed him to watch a strange surgery being performed on the mission's pickup truck. Perhaps this episode was most ostensibly responsible for the obsession that, from that time on, he had harbored for machines. Ostensibly, because from his Indigenous brothers, he had also learned another invaluable lesson as a child: that one's eyes truly registered the details of a scene only when that image blended with its twin, submerged deep down in the viewer's memory.

Thus he believed that in some moment of unfathomable origin, an equivalent scene, involving machines and parts of engines, must have happened in his past. And these mirror images, uniting perceptions barely conscious, were to constitute the basis from which his pilot's dreams would someday take flight.

The young man was barely out of adolescence when he found himself abandoned in the middle of the jungle by the men from the city. It would take him another twenty years to build and pilot his own airplane. Twenty years of hard work and persistence, blessed by occasional moments when chance had generously smiled on him.

I had the honor of being his first passenger—news that froze me in my seat as we flew over jungle as thick and remote as that which he had managed to conquer in his younger years.

"Today I'm flying officially for the first time," he shouted with pride from his seat, tipping the wings of the tiny plane over the green immensity. "Prior to that, a flight instructor kept me from harm. . . . But don't worry, I have since had plenty of practice flying solo. . . ."

I couldn't find the strength to offer him my congratulations. We flew on in silence for another half hour, until a fork of lightning flashed close by, followed suddenly by a thunderclap exploding almost on top of us. In a few minutes, visibility went quickly down to zero.

"That's flying in the Amazon for you," he commented. We were barely two yards apart, separated by a torn curtain, he in the tiny cockpit, I in the only available passenger seat, the others having been removed to make room for the cargo.

At one point, the fear that squeezed my stomach tighter and tighter gave way to stupefaction. A hard jerk of the plane had loosened from a hook in the fuselage what seemed to be a bundle of cotton. At my feet, the pale folds of cloth gradually came apart, revealing two half-open eyes, surrounded by curly hair, which, tossed by the turbulence, looked strangely alive. I was looking at the small cadaver of a little girl, which rolled from one side to the other at the mercy of the storm jostling the aircraft.

That small body swathed like a mummy, our blind flight over the treetops, the prospect of disappearing in the middle of the jungle without a trace—all this converged to focus a singular intensity on the moment. "Who is it?" I managed to yell, not recognizing the hoarse voice coming from my own throat.

"The girl?" he screamed back, after a quick glance behind him, as if the rest of the cargo might hide other surprises. He was scared, too, I realized from the tone of his voice. The clouds around us grew denser.

Still, he started talking about the girl almost compulsively. He told me her left leg had been chewed off below the knee by an alligator, and it had been impossible to staunch the bleeding. He also said that, delirious, the little girl continued to see the alligator working its way up her thigh, its cold eyes fixed on hers. Her last wish was to be buried on solid ground. A luxury for someone who lived on the river, he added by way of explanation. As he was a friend of her parents, he was doing them this favor, making sure the child was buried in a Christian cemetery.

Without transition, he spoke to me of his boyhood spent

fishing on the Amazonian mud banks, and how this experience had served him well when he started working for the tourists, from whom be received five dollars per alligator captured alive, diving at night under reflector lights in the dark waters of the Rio Negro. Thus, as the plane bumped and tossed its way through the tempest, he told me of his life, jumping from one tributary of the river, one forest, clearing, or swamp to another, traveling along the meandering course of his past with the same velocity as our little plane hurtling through the clouds.

Listening to his stories actually saved our lives, so intently did I concentrate on his words. That we didn't crash into the jungle that afternoon must have been due to my sheer faith in his narrative talent. At one point, taking advantage of a brief moment of calm, he threw me a plastic folder with half a dozen faded photos in which he appeared, fifteen years old, true to his nickname, among fat tourists from whose hands dangled small alligators and piranhas. He had worked together with a Paraguayan guide who claimed to have left his country and made his way up the continent jumping from river to river until reaching the biggest of them all.

Then he told me of Jeff, an American from Florida who had taken a month's vacation in the Amazon. If it hadn't been for Jeff, he never would have found the determination to carry out his dream—of building and flying his own airplane. The very flying machine that now seemed destined to disintegrate in midair with us and the little girl.

Fishing had brought them together, as both were expert anglers. In his small canoe, Skinny Pedro had taught Jeff to use a net and taken him far beyond Lake Ubim, where no tourist had ever been. They spent entire afternoons fishing. The American, who in the photos looked like an English explorer of the nineteenth century on a visit to Africa, was a man of few words.

But exactly three months after he left, the promise he'd made to the young guide had been honored: Through a fellow tourist, to whom he had recommended the hotel built on top of a bunch of trees, he had sent Pedro a model airplane kit.

The arrival of the small glider had probably represented the most important single event in Skinny Pedro's youth, since it gave a concrete form to his passion. For the first time, he looked at the sky with a feeling akin to possession and intimacy.

Pedro had assembled his little model plane, made entirely of pieces of fine, smooth wood—the lightest and most delicate wood he had ever seen—with the tenderness of a newlywed who, in the silence of the dawn, leans over his sleeping spouse to hear her breathe. He used the glue sparingly, for he knew it would be difficult to obtain more. Assisted by his Paraguayan friend, who also spoke a little English, he read and reread each paragraph of the instructions before carrying out their commands with a religious fervor.

But he had forgotten the monkeys. And when, at daybreak on January 15, 1972 (a date forever engraved in his memory), he had climbed the highest of the three towers built by the hotel, he failed (unlikely as it may seem) to recall the warning every guide repeated to the tourists: An inspired monkey was capable of causing as much havoc as a small elephant. And five monkeys had been present at the silent launching of the fragile glider, which should have stayed in the air for some minutes, borne on the bosom of the wind, before landing sweetly on a treetop, from which it would then be retrieved by Pedro for another flight. Two of the monkeys had applauded the event with hopping and grunts, but the other three had shot like arrows into the trees, chasing after the peculiar bird that had remained indifferent to their antics.

So Skinny Pedro had experienced the pain of seeing his

dream simultaneously realized and shattered. Each monkey had kept a piece of the little glider. And no one at the hotel had ever mentioned the incident again, out of respect for the alligator hunter's feelings.

But Pedro didn't give up. Quite the opposite. He dived into the black waters with redoubled energy, accumulating ever more generous tips—for he was the tourists' favorite—and didn't rest until he obtained from the hotel management the promise that their agent in Florida would send along another model plane with the first willing tourist—equipped this time with a cable and a small engine.

"The problem then was the macaws." Not really a problem, more of a false alarm. The macaws only wanted to inspect the intruder, as they didn't seem to feel that their territory was actually threatened. Two of them flew slightly above the small plane and its cable. Pedro had painted the model in bright colors—red, blue, and yellow—and the circular ballet of the trio against the green jungle didn't feel out of place; rather, the birds seemed to enjoy the homage being paid to them.

After some time (a time suddenly detached from our flight's duration, encapsulated as we both were in Pedro's innumerable tales), the clouds around our tiny plane began to dissolve, and the rain stopped beating forcefully on the windshield. In a corner of the cabin, the dead girl finally rested under her curls. Then a clearing and a small landing strip became visible in front of us. A few more minutes and we landed.

When the little plane stopped moving, we remained silent and motionless in our seats, exhausted but full of a precious energy bursting with relief. There was nobody to meet us; the jeep that had been scheduled to pick us up had gotten stuck about ten miles away and would take another two or three hours to arrive. Outside, fine rain continued to fall. Skinny

Pedro unfastened his seat belt and turned his seat around to face me.

"Things got ugly when the men found out the flour had spoiled," he then said. And added, as if it were necessary, "In the camp I was telling you about." The story that had been circling in his memory for years now seemed ready to alight.

The rain, or the rats, had made holes in all the flour sacks. With the high humidity, most of the stock had rotted in a few days. The foreman dragged the fellow responsible for this disaster by the hair to a corner of the encampment and, deaf to his pleas, put two bullets in his head. The prospectors, grouped on a little promontory, shuddered as they heard the shots. For the first time, they looked at the turn in the river with fear.

Pedro sensed the collective dread. His aloofness came from the certainty that he would escape, and from a feeling akin to hope that he could save his companions. Or some of them at least. But the void between certainty and hope, where the foreman ruled, troubled him. To protect them all from the violence he knew was coming, Pedro had to change things around somehow—or all would be lost.

There were other people and other camps maybe fifty miles away. But where? The skipper of one of the boats had told them something they hadn't realized, having traveled at night when they first arrived. The skipper said that just around the familiar turn, the river divided into dozens of branches, which forked and joined again and again, forming a maze so complicated that even he, with more than forty years' experience in the region, had gotten lost more than once, despite his compass and radio.

Truth? Lies? Two prospectors who had once flown over the area confirmed that, seen from above, the rivers looked like a handful of golden worms twisting through the green.

Based on these statements, the men had concluded it was

better to obey the foreman's orders and wait for the next boat. On it, representatives could be sent to the big city to negotiate the group's destiny. Leaving the camp at that point would only mean endangering everyone's fate.

Pedro scratched his chin, with his eyes *on the other turn of the river*, the one a mile and a half upstream, to the right of the camp. They said that if you went that way, you could end up in Peru. Or Ecuador. But how to navigate against the current? And for how many days? He looked at that other turn of the river, then at the generator. And he then looked at the foreman.

Two weeks went by in this fashion, the prospectors locked into a routine that became a sort of umbilical cord linking them to their past. Although they were convinced there was nothing to be found in those waters, they continued panning. They didn't even bother to spread within the area marked out by the company. Keeping together in groups, they mulled their doubts over in the ooze, their silence pierced only by the screams of birds.

Meanwhile, Pedro fished. He would take the canoe to the middle of the river and throw his net in, pulling it out almost at once with a strong jerk. When he wasn't fishing, he read.

Until, one afternoon, he stopped in front of the generator and examined it at length. Then, one last time, he began to dismantle it. But this time, his movements were slow and measured, as if he were rediscovering the weight and structure of each of its parts and seeing them from a new and secret angle.

When the men came back at nightfall, they found the components of the generator spread out on a canvas by order of size, gleaming as if they were on exhibit or possibly for sale. The men stared in silence. Fatigue, hunger, and heat kept them from articulating any thoughts.

The foreman came over to the group and asked rudely what

was going on. Pedro explained his ideas. He began by pointing to the stars. Ever since he was small, he said, he had known how to find directions by looking at the night sky. For the other prospectors, who came mostly from the northeast, the stars were a mystery, but for him they held no secrets. And since going downstream didn't seem feasible, the best thing was to go upstream. They would stop during the day, or whenever the waters forked, and proceed at night, with the help of the stars. Who knew what they might find a few miles away.

"Go upstream? Against the current?" exclaimed the foreman while sixty pair of eyes glittered around the two of them like fireflies. "How?"

Pedro pointed to the parts spread out on the canvas. "By making an engine. For the canoe." In a lower voice, he added, "You can come with me, if you trust me."

The foreman laughed. He put both hands on his hips and laughed long and loud at the full moon, his head thrown back. His whole body shook, intimidating everyone. It had been months since anyone had laughed in the camp. Suddenly, with the agility of a wild animal, he grabbed Skinny Pedro by the collar of his dirty shirt and whispered in his ear, "If the son of a bitch works, I'll go with you. If it doesn't, I'll kill you."

It would work, Pedro assured him, and got busy on it that very night.

For over two weeks he struggled, without neglecting his fishing. On the contrary, he spent long hours throwing his nets into the river and pulling them back with hard, quick tugs. Watching him, the men had the impression that he was pulling inspiration for his masterpiece directly out of the water. Every night, they all squatted around the contraption, which, to everyone's surprise, snorted and purred, sending out puffs of smoke with all the earnestness of an engine.

The fateful day arrived. They all stopped working to watch the little canoe rocking under the foreman's weight. Skinny Pedro instructed him to sit on the middle bench, facing the turn in the river, with his back to him, but steadying between his legs the gallon cans of gasoline with which they would refuel the tank. Four men, wading up to their waists in the river, held the prow fast while another four helped Skinny Pedro fasten the engine to the stern with a single solid hook. It was heavy, that machine of his! At a command from Pedro, the canoe was launched with a slow push toward the middle of the stream.

Standing, his hand resting on the silent engine, the first machine for which he felt truly responsible, Skinny Pedro wore a fishnet over one shoulder. It fanned outward over the bottom of the canoe, giving him the singular appearance of a gladiator. The foreman sat in the middle of the canoe, both hands on the bench. He studied the muddy waters in front of them as he waited for the morning silence to be filled by the roar of the engine.

Quickly, the miracle occurred—and the engine amply fulfilled the collective dream of the men gathered on the bank. With a lightning-speed motion, Pedro tossed a cord around the foreman's neck. With another, he threw the fishnet over him. The engine, freed from its hook by a sudden hard, precise kick, quickly sank into the river, pulling the cord tight and dragging the foreman underwater. The canoe turned over; Pedro disappeared. For a few seconds the foreman struggled, strangled under the fishnet, making a few hoarse, stilled gurgling noises from below the surface, but soon he disappeared, too. And Skinny Pedro resurfaced from under the upside-down canoe.

Absolute silence descended on the scene. Men and birds watched Skinny Pedro swimming after the oars, as if his slow arm strokes could help them decipher the mystery they had all just witnessed. His movements through the mild current were tranquil, as if he were the author and master, not only of the sequence of events but of the very landscape around them.

Once he recovered both oars, he righted the canoe and climbed into it again. Standing up, he shook his frizzy hair back into the wind and turned to look at the prospectors. One of them, fist raised to the sky, let out a long yell, the hoarse shout of a gold panner. Then they all shouted, jumping up and down in the mud, throwing their shovels into the river. Many hugged and kissed one another.

Skinny Pedro had conquered for each man in the camp the sacred right to choose how to confront his own death. Staying or leaving. Struggling through the jungle on foot or building rafts. And since he had been unable to share the secret with any of them before, he now savored these screams with the joy of one who bends fate to his own will.

When the rain stopped, I felt the need to take a few steps on solid ground. The same solid ground Pedro had mentioned when talking of the dead little girl. To celebrate this luxury of sorts, I accepted the straw cigarette he offered me. Smoking in the dripping jungle, I learned, by way of an epilogue, how half the prospectors had followed him down the river in rafts tied by ropes—and how they had been saved, after wandering through the green labyrinth for weeks on end. As for the other half, nobody ever knew what became of them.

The Magic Eye

Part I

1

The man sits at his desk once again in search of his sentence, like a ship seeking a lighthouse in the dead of night. He knows he has a story to tell—and that, *somewhere,* a sentence awaits. This certainty is all he needs.

As usual, he hesitates. Then his mind drifts back to the interview he had given a few hours earlier. The young reporter had asked where his stories came from. And he'd replied, "From a sentence." The interviewer had smiled and proclaimed, "But every work of fiction does that."

This caused him to regard the reporter with sincere envy, as he recalled his own days of certainties powered by irony (or of ironies fed by uncertainties).

To the young man, however, he'd merely spoken the truth. Because everything did, in fact, begin with a sentence—followed by the abyss. Hence the blank stares that usually met his statements: No one else knew anything about the abyss.

He turns his attention to a recent scene that suddenly strikes him as odd. It concerned something utterly ordinary: a simple tube of toothpaste. He'd thrown it into the wrong bin, which his wife had noticed, promptly informing him, "It's not recyclable—it's ordinary trash."

Ordinary trash, ordinary man—what kind of categories would these terms fit into, he'd asked himself, without knowing exactly where to file that particular question. His wife, however, had persisted. With a sharp "Furthermore," she'd offered a preview of what was yet to come: Squeezed to its limit, the poor tube had revealed, in the bathroom sink, just how much toothpaste it still contained. So it was that, peaceful and resigned, the tube and the man had exchanged looks: the former calm, maybe even relieved, given its status as an inanimate object; the latter enlightened yet subjected to the assorted domestic lessons targeted at him each day; and, in between the two, the pragmatic wife, who had done no more than make evident a given of real life.

He was tired of fighting against these moments of routine domesticity, which in previous times would have gone unremarked but now were unceremoniously and persistently inserted into his life—despite their complete irrelevance.

Things from long ago had gone the way of the horse and carriage, as his mother used to say at one of those times when she'd succumb to melancholy spells, evincing a special fondness for the customs and fashions of a forgotten era. Inevitably, now, he focused on his predicament, for he and his wife had been holed up at home for at least eight consecutive months, forgotten like characters in a discarded play, a situation that led him to speculate about his mother's horse and carriage: *Where could they possibly have gone?* Here he smiled, as no one in the building would ever deal with such matters, let alone have the answer to how long their present ordeal would last.

In his case, this meant being patient, and enduring endless days of cleaning bathrooms, vacuuming, deciphering TV series, washing pots and pans, all in an atmosphere that became less breathable by the day, leading him to assume there must be plenty of neighbors who'd surmise that the couple was struggling—friendly neighbors, who might come to discuss how the current extraordinary circumstances were affecting the building's older tenants.

Such concerns might well have gotten back to the super, causing him to scratch his head pensively before remarking to his wife sympathetically, "People are looking out for the old folks in eight oh two"—because he was sensitive to issues that gave rise to helplessness or solitude.

Confinement . . . This topic didn't help the writer with his efforts, either. It was too abstract, in a way that relegated the quarantine to the nightly news, where it had no competition and dominated the scene—in a repetitive and uninteresting way.

A paradox perhaps, but it didn't intrigue him. For there was nothing on TV that related to the unknown—and after months of the same old spectacle, not even death was surprising anymore. True, the numbers grew. But wasn't that expected of them?

What would warrant reporting—and generate interest?

A line by a French writer came to mind. A hundred years ago, at one of his soirées, he had declared that there was nothing more stimulating, for a storyteller, than coming upon two words: *And then?*

In his case, he couldn't even consider the question, because there was no *before*.

So then, nothing.

He recalled the suggestion he'd given one of his editors, a man whose wonder at him bordered on doubt, when he'd proposed publishing a volume made up of blank pages—except for the first, which, on its last line, after proclaiming everything to the four winds, would abruptly go silent.

"Readers would all rush to the cash register, demanding their money back!" his editor had objected, laughing. "Yes, but in perfect symmetry with the work's intensity," he'd replied without batting an eye, "the women pale, the men livid, all mirrored in the emptiness of the pages and stung by their reflections."

All hoping someone . . .

Would teach them a thing or two
about how many sticks
would make a good canoe . . .

. . . as went the nursery rhyme his father sometimes recited to him in his childhood—raising his bushy eyebrows all the while, for he was a man who cultivated figurative language, often adorning it with imagined italics.

Maybe by joining or deleting phrases but retaining the essentials from the whole, he might finally come up with his sentence?

Things from long ago had gone the way of the horse and carriage, without it being possible to determine whether a father's nursery rhyme would teach anyone a thing or two about how many sticks would make a good canoe.

It was a beginning, like any other. More outlandish than most, but far inferior paragraphs had already rendered him a book or two. Without much enthusiasm, he prepared to forge ahead—when the doorbell rang.

Saved by the bell, he mused, again instantly transported back to his childhood and the myriad sounds that accompanied it, bells and chimes alternating with other tones. Gongs in particular always held his attention, as they seemed to resonate longest in some mysterious realm that competed with light and life itself. So strong was the association that he jotted down *gong* on a pad kept near his laptop. And he jauntily headed toward the door to see who, heedlessly disregarding the public health advisories, dared to disturb them. Any help to his text would be welcome, naturally. But he made his way to the door not in search of aid—much less inspiration—for he was now buoyed by the image of that musical intruder and the wealth of possibilities it represented.

The gong was, after all, an interesting and versatile instrument, renowned for its many uses. Take the luxurious transatlantic vessels that once upon a time traversed oceans, and consider their first-class passengers—the gentlemen in tailcoats, the ladies in ball gowns and gloves—all of them summoned to dinner by the sound of a shiny bronze disk struck by a steward in a spotless white uniform with gold buttons, a man who strode with marked dignity along the decks, producing his singular notes every ten paces or so.

Could this have been the steward's primary role and reason for being aboard the enormous ship? Certainly he did much more during the day, but nothing that so clearly dictated the daily routines of the majestic vessel—or even his own, inasmuch as he controlled the fate of that particular sample of humanity by presiding over their individual appetites.

These were his thoughts as he passed by his wife's room and heard her say, "Are you going to get it? Don't open the door before checking who it is."

He sailed across a sea of whitecaps, rug by rug, on the way to the door, amused by his wife's totally dispensable advice. They'd lived in that apartment for years and not once had the door ever been opened without the visitor's being inspected beforehand through the tiny peephole—which they still lovingly referred to as "the magic eye."

Just his luck to be lost amid such musings—and, therefore, distracted—when he peered through the peephole and saw a blurry figure that could be taken a number of ways.

"Who is it?" he inquired.

"Dong-dong!"

The gong?

The very one . . . and suggestive of a life preserver that, after emerging from the depths of the Atlantic, had landed on his deck, covered in algae, plankton, and saltiness, to rescue him and offer an alternative for his text. Only one question intrigued him now: Would the reality on the other side of the door permeate his fiction?

If so, to what end?

Here he thought of the advice given by a great film director to one of his protégés, to the effect that, when shooting interior scenes, it was always worth leaving a door open, to sustain the viewer's illusion that someone might enter through it. And right then, a man *did come* onto his set, announcing, as if by magic, the unfolding not so much of the plot as of the scene.

A nurse in uniform, no less, who moved with the fervor of a military man. In a matter of minutes, acting on a request made a month earlier by the couple (and since then completely forgotten by both), he vaccinated the two, completed the pertinent medical paperwork, and, slipping his shoes back on at the door, exclaimed, "Congratulations! The flu is killing people left and right. Almost as many as the pandemic."

So he was saved by the gong. Promoted to a paragraph, his sentence had gained a new companion and, with it, a shot of enthusiasm that heralded new changes:

As if by magic, the gong had rung once again. Having gone the way of the horse and carriage, however, it would cease to be heard, without it being possible to proclaim to the four winds a thing or two about how many sticks would make a good canoe.

2

The man *knows* he has a story to tell. But he remains ignorant as to which. Instead of relying on his sentence, however, he now clings to his carriage. With it, he reckons, he might stand a chance of getting somewhere.

He senses the carriage had approached the inn slowly because the final stretch of the road had been encumbered by a succession of climbs, some steep, as well as by the rain, which had beaten down all afternoon on the travelers and animals alike.

An hour goes by. The carriage is now stopped in front of the entrance to the inn. Two of the four horses, tossing their manes beneath the moonlight, are beginning to show signs of impatience. The coachman, in blue cap and uniform, has just returned from a quick trip to the stable, where, having no other option, he had relieved himself in a dark corner.

If the hay bales could talk, they might have vented their indignation, not only those drenched and humiliated by the poor coachman's pressing needs but also those trampled and crushed by the pudgy knees of the cook, who, mounted by the servant that afternoon, had taken advantage of a work break to satisfy a portion of her desires.

Good thing her husband was busy readying the bedrooms, she had thought while buttoning her blouse, somewhat concerned to know if her soup was salty or if the meat she'd spent hours preparing was still roasting in the sizable oven without being overdone.

Leaning against the carriage, the driver concentrates on gnawing the mutton leg the innkeeper had sent him along with a generous cup of red wine and an unexpected apple. In a few minutes, he and his passengers would be undertaking the final leg of their journey. Should the rain hold off, they'd reach their destination in two hours. Satisfied at the prospect, the man tosses the bone and licks his fingers before wiping them on his trousers.

Life was beautiful.

So, too, for different reasons, thought the six guests drinking near the inn hearth, pleased with the flames that warmed their bodies, weary from the long journey, giving them all strength to discuss topics of the day, among them the rumors that Austrian troops were approaching from the border.

Outside, the air might smell of gunpowder, but in the coziness of the common room, peace and harmony reigned. Just what ideas or principles the men would go back to killing in the name of, none knew for certain—in part because the aromas wafting from the kitchen filled their nostrils and the promise of the meal to come kept them united in a sea of optimism.

All they had to do was savor their Burgundy and celebrate the impending arrival of the nineteenth century. What a time they lived in! And how lucky they were to still have a head on their shoulders, when so many had been guillotined, to drumrolls, on the country's public squares in the past decade. For how much longer, the more disquieted asked themselves, would the map of Europe be redrawn?

They were all middle-aged men, *citoyens de la République*, bourgeois at heart and merchants by trade. They had no way of associating the shadows dancing on the walls behind the semicircle of their seats with myths of bygone times—even though these had everything to do with the crossroads they now found themselves at.

How to understand a reality that was at once close yet distant? And therefore inaccessible? If they were all bound, not to a cave, but to that room—and saw nothing beyond the recent atrocities, which would be reenacted relentlessly over the subsequent two centuries? At the end of which their descendants would raise the same questions, convinced, every generation, that they had changed or evolved, when essentially nothing around them had budged an inch?

"What was that cry?" one of the guests suddenly exclaims. "Outside . . . Did you hear it?"

3

The cry was yet to be heard in the night. For now, silence prevails, in which a heartbroken peasant examines his canoe. A rock had split the side of the fragile vessel. Listing as it took on water, the small boat hadn't completely sunk because it was tied to a tree, right where he'd left it the night before—as he did every evening, without its ever having been the target of theft or vandalism.

What a shame, that rock ... Big and round, the size of a cannonball, it had put an end to one of his most cherished pastimes.

No more fishing in the middle of the lagoon or at the mouth of the upper river—or at least not for a long while. He wasn't sure just how much wood would go into his canoe nor where he'd find it in the area. Not to mention his lack of resources for such.

But the worst was yet to come: He now has no choice but to spend his nights with his wife, stuck in their hut and forced to give up the discoveries made during those hours of solitude, after which he'd arrive home with no fish in his sack, but steeped in dreams.

He looks up at the sky and sees the full moon. He beholds the forest to his right, from which he's never seen a single soul emerge, and notes with surprise that two shadows are moving between the trees, strange figures lit by a lantern, one of them a woman in a white nightshirt.

Startled, he watches the scene. He sees clearly that the man, heavyset and strong, carries an ax on his shoulder—a lumberjack, he imagines. The woman doesn't seem to be accompanying him willingly—she actually walks in front, as if prodded by him. She stumbles and pauses, her fear evident with each step.

Even from a distance, he can tell that the lumberjack is at least a head taller than he is and has the added advantage of the ax; all the peasant can count on is the rusty knife he uses on bait.

He hears horses whinnying in the distance, eager to depart. *The inn . . .* He'd certainly find help there, maybe even a weapon. *But to what end?* By the time he got back, the lumberjack would have disappeared into the forest, absconding with his terrified prey, whose muffled whimpering he now hears.

To deter the violence he believes inevitable, he then cries out into the still of the night. In response, however, he hears only the wind that, in a sudden gust, sweeps over the treetops.

Looking back at the forest, he sees nothing but shadows.

4

Scenes that come and go among so many others . . .

A half dozen lost souls at an inn on the cusp of a now distant century—whose worries had gone the way of the horse and carriage long ago. The anonymous cry of a peasant who dreams of his fish in the still of the night—and whose helplessness might be as real and intense as . . .

"A glass of water?" asks his wife, cracking open the door.

A glass of water. She rarely interrupts him, but he doesn't seem bothered, as he often approaches writing as a composer would, and can still hear his words safely suspended in the air like a refrain. He takes the water and thanks his spouse as she leaves.

Now, where was I? Oh yes, in the still of the night . . .

He enjoys wordplay. And appreciates the richness of working with a language full of verbal innuendos. In no other tongue, as far as he knows, does the night allow for a term that moves even as it conveys stillness.

The nocturnal silence adds to his cabin fever. Cloistered at home by order of public authorities, grappling with his text, wed to every word, he faces a perfect storm in a glass of water. How could he not thank his wife for the interruption, which had brought to reality a new sense of urgency?

Moreover, these are the plots that bring him pleasure. And

interest him, with their crossroads and allusions. But they also end up being the ones that worry his editors. Not to mention his translators, who at times must contend with paragraphs difficult to convey in their dominant languages.

Poor dominant languages . . .

As an homage to them, he cautiously goes back to his text:

As if by magic, the gong had sounded again, this time in the still of the night. However, it would soon cease to be heard, leaving in its wake a sinking feeling so common among abandoned manuscripts—and canoes vulnerable to missing wood, vandalism, and wars.

5

A few weeks before the pandemic, at the suggestion of his wife—who was following advice from her psychic—they'd traded bedrooms.

They'd slept in separate rooms for a long time without realizing that neither benefited, in Madame Vandá's somewhat solemn words, from "the harmony needed for restorative sleep." This problem, as the psychic saw it, stemmed from the elusive field of their vital energies.

Vital or not, the room swap had brought well-being—to the extent that he'd even considered consulting Madame Vandá about his manuscripts. But studying himself closely in the mirror while shaving a few days later, he'd changed his mind.

Any number of reasons had led to their sleeping for so many years in what were, according to the insightful woman, "the wrong rooms." ("How can you dream?" she'd asked.) Except that they didn't remember those reasons and had no way of assessing how that setup might have affected their lives.

His wife's dreams, in fact, had been taking on unknown dimensions lately, as she never referred to this aspect of her inner journeys. There was no record of her remarking, the way couples or friends so often did to each other, "Last night I had a curious dream," or, more commonly, "the strangest dream."

Certainly she dreamed. . . . But she seemed to have lost the keys to that secret domain of hers. He'd thought about suggesting that she seek help but soon gave up. He knew from experience that, in her case, therapy would be viable only if magic were involved.

A magician . . . Why not? If her mind tended toward mystery, nothing more natural than entrusting it to a professional familiar with the uncanny. Someone for whom the unexpected didn't necessarily conceal an enigma but, rather, an illusion, a simple trick . . .

From among his thoughts, a biblical image came to mind—the fall of the walls of Jericho. Bolstered by a seer, on the one hand, and a magician, on the other, he convinced himself that behind those majestic walls, metaphorical or not, was hidden whatever his wife refused to reveal—not as much to him as to herself.

If the wall came down, he thought, *she would dream.*

And he would gain entry to her fortress. After all, wasn't he the one who had been rooting for the implosion of those walls, the toppling and crumbling of tons of rock mixed with mud and clay—forever blessed by the waters of the Jordan River?

Now, after so many months of seclusion, he continued to await his wife's dreaming behind that hallowed fortification.

The ancient walls, the solid walls of Jericho, he sometimes murmured, eyeing the barrier that separated his bedroom from his wife's quarters. For he didn't fear the ridicule, and even indulged in situations that made a mockery of reality.

Then, one night, the door had cracked open, and his wife had appeared in front of him—so unexpectedly that at first he'd been startled. It was barely five in the morning.

"I saw the light on," she'd said by way of apology.

He'd smiled to put her at ease. Her eyes shined; her hair was tousled.

"I wanted to tell you," she'd continued, taking two steps toward him, "about the dream I just had."

Praised be the gods and their apostles, he'd had the strength to think, before disappearing beneath an avalanche of earth, clay, and rocks that brought down age-old walls and buried him completely as he, perhaps the most awake of sleepwalkers, surrendered to the waters of the Jordan River.

6

They settled in the living room, a kind of neutral ground where they sometimes met, as if, every so often, to confer a certain seriousness on what was being discussed.

Typically, these gatherings almost always took place when a mutual acquaintance departed, which would lead them to grieve a bit and then reminisce about some experience they'd shared with the deceased. On these occasions, they never failed to congratulate each other on their excellent state of health.

In any event, the resonance of their words, in that atmosphere, heightened their sense of reality. As if they carefully ruminated their lines before digesting them. Whatever they lost in subtleties or digressions, they gained in density.

"Would you like some water?" he asked, interested in the dream but preoccupied with his texts, which he'd just left on their own.

Oblivious to his offer, Eva began her recounting. "In the dream, the super came to see us. He sat in one of the upholstered chairs."

He steadied himself to contain his incredulity. "The super!" He refused to tread on the ruins of her wall at the hands of such an unqualified guide.

She pointed with her index finger at the piece of furniture to the right of the sofa they were sitting on.

"In the blue armchair."

He had turned on only one of the two lamps. As such, they remained enveloped in shadows. He got up, turned on the second lamp, and looked at the blue armchair, as if he could conjure the figure who, a short time before, had sat three feet away from them. Not that he disliked the young man; quite the opposite.

But honestly, dreaming about the super!

He felt frustrated. In her honor, he'd put up nothing less than the walls of Jericho . . . and even managed to bring them down! Not even Cleopatra could have aspired to so much.

It was a fleeting sensation, however, and he soon regained his composure. A few moments passed, during which he closed his eyes. His wife's initial statements suggested a story of no importance.

She went on with her telling. And he learned that he'd been taking his usual after-lunch nap when the intercom had buzzed. Eva had answered and, sensing that the matter seemed urgent, decided to let the super come up, certain that his visit had to do with the building.

Upon realizing that she would be the one seeing him, the super had asked after her husband. He wasn't actually annoyed but seemed visibly preoccupied. So much so that he proceeded to explain himself. As if . . .

. . . there was no time to lose.

He didn't need words to follow her train of thought. That she knew how to craft a story wasn't news to him. Besides being an excellent photographer, she'd been a journalist. *Even so, her dream sounded so well-documented, transmitted little by little and with such surgical precision. . . .*

Yet, it wasn't a narrative that brought his wife relief, he also began to notice, much less pleasure. Rather, it suggested some sort of pressing need. As if she were spawning her images.

He was intrigued by the language he'd resorted to. Fish and turtles spawn their offspring, successful films spawn sequels. . . . But dreams?

And where had the unease that was already emerging come from?

They were seated side by side on the sofa, which led him to study her profile. He noticed that she'd smoothed her hair into place and spruced herself up a bit.

The narrative of the super had gradually resumed. Summoned by the doorman, he'd gone down to talk to a family who had taken refuge in the building's garage. They had a little girl in tow. And a suitcase. It was an urgent matter—a crisis of sorts.

They needed help. With the streets practically deserted on account of the pandemic, the three of them were suddenly all too visible. "What about the police?" she had asked the super. "That's who they're trying to get away from," came the reply. "The police *and* the drug dealers."

The man glanced at the empty armchair again. Police, drug dealers . . . Things were going from bad to worse. He noticed that day was breaking outside. The birds were beginning to rehearse the daily cacophony that would soon overtake the streets.

"How about some orange juice?" he asked his wife, who still didn't seem to hear him.

It was a real emergency, the super had insisted. Thus his search for someone who could shelter the family for a day or so. He'd honed in on the three apartments housing only two tenants. One of them was undergoing renovations and the owners were absent. Of the remaining two, he had first appealed to the couple in 401. Embarrassed, he'd admitted, "They hung up on me in a huff."

The man could hardly follow what he was hearing. Everything sounded so natural. . . . The refugees in the garage, the indignant couple from 401, the super's visit to his wife, and now, the two of them discussing the dream—each playing a role in their respective capacities. But like puppets. Not to mention that nothing made sense. . . . He was lost in the story the way he sometimes disappeared between the lines of his manuscripts. What was it all about? A dream, of course, nonsense . . . Dreams were like that.

Or weren't they?

Remembering the embarrassment she had detected in the super's words from the start, his wife finally explained, in the same tone the visitor had used with her—lower, almost a whisper—that the family was Black.

"*Black?*" the writer repeated.

"Yes. That's what the super said." And then, as if it were necessary, she hastened to add, "In the dream."

It made sense, the man thought, pausing briefly on the care with which the issue of race had been introduced.

When he'd turned his attention back to his wife's story, though, the family was already inside *their* apartment. The girl, clinging to her mother's legs, stared at Eva. The super had vanished.

"Then I woke up."

The man was miffed by the sudden ending. His wife hadn't even bothered to bow before exiting the scene. That ending had sounded oddly unexpected—as though she'd broken a secret rule by waking up without his permission.

And now, she had left him alone, locked in her dream.

Alone with a family of strangers in his apartment. Without his knowing what to make of the three of them—much less of the story.

Adding another dimension to his bewilderment, Eva had whispered, "I can't stop thinking about the girl."

7

The girl. He had hardly thought of her. . . . Whereas his wife had been moved nearly to tears when she had concluded her saga.

As for him—he recalled sheepishly—upon learning of the family, he'd gotten hung up on the suitcase. *What might it hold? And what might be causing the family to be pursued?*

Unlike him, she had focused on the girl. That was the nature of the distance separating them. It hadn't always been that way, though.

They'd met spraying graffiti on buildings five decades earlier and had gone on to defend the many kinds of causes that had inspired and motivated their generation. If they'd had children, those kids would have been proud of them.

Now, however, at his wife's doing, the child filled with her presence the space she had been brought into. And a burst of beauty swept through the apartment, injecting the stark environment with the vitality that emanated from the girl's existence—while providing the dream with a renewed density.

So thought the writer as he considered the story's thread from his wife's point of view. He felt at least partly responsible for what had happened—after all, he'd created, with his ancient walls, the circumstances that had given rise to the plot they now found themselves immersed in.

Still, his wife had been the one to dream. And, by dreaming, she'd led the child to her fate. Rather than being concerned, however, he was interested. To buy time, he thought to downplay the moment. To be able to better deal with it later. (*When Eva truly woke up,* he thought.)

And then?

Expert at reading his thoughts, she replied, "Then, nothing."

"Nothing?"

"Nothing."

He noticed she was downcast. Her visions had been intense; she'd lived the dream as reality. It was almost as if, having in some measure been adopted, the girl was now seated between them. Without her parents, without the super. Only her.

Yet, little by little, the child's presence began to fade, despite the onset of daylight. Or because of it. That's when Eva's silence again weighed heavily.

End of the narrative, he surmised.

But not of the story, he also understood. It wasn't over, nor would it be. Walls didn't come down without leaving vestiges behind—from legends to mythology, from the bedrocks of faith to the fundamentals of science, from wars to revolutions.

Faced with his wife's silence, he persisted. "But what did *you* think? About this journey of yours?"

And, once again, Eva surprised him. "Why didn't we ever talk about adoption?"

8

Over the course of the day, they chose not to return to the topic, each for their own reasons. (He would've given anything to know hers.) One thing was for certain, though: The experience had worn them out. Eva had gone back to sleep and didn't wake up until the afternoon; he'd returned to his room and puttered there without reading or writing anything. He felt anxious.

Most of all—and to his astonishment—he felt irrelevant. Because the dream had swept aside the few pages he'd written in recent days, negotiating each turn, each detour, connecting with difficulty images that hardly went together, stories that spoke a language other than his own. The dream had cast his manuscript aside.

Outside, a flesh-and-blood reality existed. In which people died or vanished in the blink of an eye. And compared to which his literature paled.

He was being hard on himself, of course. And needed to relax. Like most older people, he was somewhat paranoid. (Like all writers, he appreciated a hint of paranoia.) Still, that was how he felt: insecure.

The abyss was closing in on him. Gradually but decisively. In his apartment before and after the dream. In his conscience ever since.

Upon waking, his wife had rescued the child. But she hadn't done it out of some instinctive or maternal reaction. In her mind, that was exactly where the story got its strength from.

And him? What was he thinking, perched atop his personal Olympus?

About his work. His own little world.

But something new had happened: He was now contending with questions that assailed him *as a character*, not an author.

In this context, he'd gained a new perspective, with which he'd reexamined his writings. But going through them had not brought the expected pleasure. He found nothing reflected, in relevance, beauty, and intensity, the force of the little girl's gaze at Eva as she clung to her mother, sensing her father drenched in a cold sweat two steps away.

And then?

And then, he asked himself how many Blacks there would have been on his ocean liner who weren't working in the engine rooms or galleys of the luxurious vessel. He wondered if any of them would have heard, albeit from afar, the ringing of the steward's gong—or even caught a glimpse of the elegant staterooms.

On the other hand, he knew just where those figures stood when the *citoyens de la République française*, on the cusp of a new century, celebrated their liberty, equality, and fraternity: on the plantations of the three Americas, French plantations among them, in the West Indies, laboring at impossible and debilitating jobs from dawn to dusk, after having been chained like animals on one side of the ocean to be sold like cattle on the other, where they would suffer the most degrading atrocities.

Question after question—and he asked himself many that afternoon—he kept coming back to his wife. (And he came unsettled, stepping on eggshells.) Could she have rested after setting fire to her gunpowder magazine? Having spawned her dream, would she now sleep in peace? Leaving him alone amid the turmoil?

He found himself far from the beauty she had created by bringing the child into their orbit. Caught up in his own world, he was little more than a bystander, lost in the background.

Nothing happened by chance, the psychic had said, even less so when dreams were concerned. One needed only to be aware of the ties that linked the images. Once these links were understood, the images became clear. . . .

It was the editing that mattered, he realized. It was the editing that had allowed the little girl to take over the scene.

Five years old . . . The age when children open up to magic. Or succumb to tragedy. It hardly mattered that the little girl didn't exist as a real live person in the broader sense of the word. *One woman had believed in her.*

That had been enough. To trust . . . An outcome that, preserving three human beings, had honored all others.

When the links were understood, the images became clear.

They were ties of compassion. His wife had dreamed. It had now fallen to him to bring the dream to life. By taking the alchemy to its final stages. And by availing himself of his writing.

Would he be up to the challenge?

For the first time, then, he took a deep breath. Between no-man's-land and the promised land, he was at a loss for words. But he no longer felt alone, isolated in the background. Who, if not him, could come up with the perfect synthesis that would let the story be told?

He took another deep breath. A feeling of well-being took over and inspired him. The time had come. And so, with a light heart, he wrote:

As if by magic, the elderly couple in 802 had set fire to their gunpowder and denounced to the four winds the lesser beings of 401. Having done so, they had exposed to the world the lowlifes around them, teaching these minor creatures a thing or two about how many sticks would make a good canoe, whether said vessel was leaking or not, sinking or not (like the forgotten texts of a certain author), accompanied or not by the singular notes of a gong, ringing nonstop in the still of the night to celebrate the hard-won emancipations yet to come around the world, one after the other, to the sound of violins, harps, and barrel drums; in the supreme understanding that, on a curve of a clay road, an elegant carriage would slow its pace, in time to allow the coachman to fire a sure musket shot at the heavyset lumberjack's forehead and, with a flourish of his right arm, turn all dreams into reality, to general astonishment, lifting from the ground, in one swift move, like a feather, the trembling and beautiful damsel in the white nightshirt, whose flowing tresses would cascade down the shoulder of her savior, cooling him with the dew of the forest and giving off scents that would lead our improbable hero to proclaim loudly and definitively that, yes, life was beautiful and—by God!—they would all one day step on eggshells as they entered paradise.

Part II

9

They almost always had lunch in the eat-in nook near the kitchen and the small veranda, where, per doctor's orders, he basked in the sun for exactly fifteen minutes each morning. (He had something in common with his steward, beyond his fascination with ocean liners: a weakness for precision.)

The intercom was located near the veranda. And it had buzzed while they were having dessert. *A delivery of some sort?*

He answered. It was the super. The man saw his wife blanch. He instinctively turned his back to her and exchanged a few brief words with the super.

"All right," he said before hanging up.

He sat back down and cut a slice of cheese to go with the guava paste already on his plate. His wife remained silent. The enormity of what had just happened didn't escape them.

The super had been at once spare with his words and enigmatic about his intentions.

"He said he'd like to come up. To discuss something."

Her look was hardly indifferent. But it served a strategic and defensive purpose, like that which occurs in tennis or volleyball games: blocking what might be coming from the other side of the net.

"I arranged for him to come at five this afternoon."

His wife also stuck to the basics. "This time, you meet with him."

The writer held back and, taking a deep breath, agreed.

This time?

It was 2:00 P.M. In the hours before the meeting, they'd go their own ways, dodging unwanted collisions in the winding corridor. In this game filled with precautions and nuances, the bedrooms were sacred and inviolable, and the living room was to be avoided. Given that they wouldn't be back in the kitchen until evening, the problem came down to the bathrooms. There were two, one a full bath, the other a powder room. He imagined that, by mutual agreement, they'd put off their respective showers.

To put his mind at rest, he came up with a bland question, of little consequence: Had the super, upon hanging up, smiled at his own wife and said gently, "Those old folks in eight-oh-two . . ."? With the notion, he sought comfort against the incipient feeling of unease.

Once lunch was over, he cleared the table and washed the dishes.

"Would you like coffee?" he asked.

"No, thanks," his wife replied, leaving the table.

He followed her with his eyes. Had she entered the living room, a conversation would inevitably have ensued. He sighed with relief as she disappeared down the hallway. And he got started on the dishes.

In recent months, he'd found doing the dishes rather enjoyable. There, at the kitchen sink, in the midst of water, sponges, and detergents, he worked through his story lines and characters. It was unfortunate that the sink didn't have a deeper basin, because his wife dirtied quite a few pots and pans, operating in that scant space with the lavishness of a master chef who deigned to cook in a provincial restaurant.

But, on second thought, and considering kinder moments that sometimes brought them joy, *how utterly boring their life had become.* . . . There was nothing wrong with their routines, other than that they were repeated ad nauseam. The problem was different—and difficult to grasp. But it existed nonetheless.

His characters no longer bathed in his sink, now filled by impersonal suds. What could be worrying him? What might his wife be thinking about right then? Could she be anxious? Calm?

Could she be dreaming about the girl again?

10

The super had been on time, arriving promptly at 5:00 P.M. After greeting him, the writer had sat on the sofa, leaving his guest to choose one of the upholstered chairs. The young man had avoided the blue one. Out of respect for his wife's dream, the host chose to disregard the issue.

But he'd noticed one detail: In the living room, which was spacious but not large, they were seated quite close to each other, a situation likely to bring an added intimacy to their conversation.

Before either could say a word, however, Eva came in with a tray of coffee. Her husband tried to disguise his surprise with a smile, behind which the super detected a hint of discomfort—a perception Eva did away with quite naturally.

"A cup of coffee hits the spot this time of day."

"I hope I'm not interrupting you this late in the afternoon," said the super.

Seated beside her husband on the sofa, the woman reassured their guest. "Not at all."

Still intrigued by her presence, her husband added, "You're not really interrupting. We were expecting you."

Here, however, his tone shifted: "But, to be honest . . ." And he continued: "I didn't get to finish rewatching *Il Gattopardo* on TV. There were five minutes left when the doorbell rang."

"*The Leopard*," his wife translated. "A film he loves."

"But don't worry, we have the DVD," the husband explained. "I can rewatch the ending later."

Bypassing the barrage of information, the guest went straight to the point. "It's one of my favorites, too."

The couple could hardly contain their glee. But without meaning to, they laid it on thick. Remarks such as "You don't say" alternated with "What a coincidence" and "Unbelievable." Which led the super to ask politely, "Why?"

Husband and wife exchanged glances. And it fell to the husband to assume the role of the Prince of Salina, the film's main character, to get them out of the awkward situation. Other than his wife, few people would have been able to tell whether he'd chosen his words with care or irony. He certainly took on the Prince's forthright and sometimes rude manner:

"Why . . . because, my man, with due respect to your being an engineer, not to mention your position as building superintendent, for which we have the utmost regard . . ."

(Too bad only a drop of lukewarm coffee was left to drink in counterpoint to the slight pause he indulged in.)

". . . I don't imagine there's another person your age in this country today who's seen Luchino Visconti's *Il Gattopardo* in its original version."

With a nervous little laugh, his wife stepped swiftly into the scene. "My husband is prone to"—she took a moment to muster courage—"exaggeration."

Gratified and relieved, the three laughed. The husband, who would have sulked at "preposterous statements," had magnanimously accepted "exaggeration"—a formulation that the super, too, took well, further smoothing the situation by mentioning that as the grandson of Italians, from Sicily, in fact, his father had made him read Lampedusa in the original when he was younger. Moreover, he'd had his son watch the same film adaptation by Visconti that they were discussing. Which he'd greatly admired.

Here the super leaned in toward the couple to convey his personal interest "in stories involving decadent aristocrats dying amid worlds of splendor."

"Excuse me," his host said, interrupting, "it's quite the opposite. There's nothing decadent about Don Fabrizio. What's decadent is the world around him! He's splendor personified. A true prince. The last of his line."

"My husband is passionate about that film," his wife interjected gently before heading off toward the kitchen.

"One of the finest screen adaptations," she heard her husband pronouncing from afar.

It was a statement that required a good pause. And, indeed, upon returning with her tray and three glasses of water, Eva caught the super's reply: "It makes its way from opera to film, by way of literature."

Resettled on the sofa, the woman reminded the others: "The health officials advise that we stay hydrated."

Once the glasses were distributed, it was up to the writer to affirm: "Both the film and the book represent a kind of mourning for a lost past. In this sense, they both evoke Proust."

No one seemed surprised that the very heart of Visconti's and Lampedusa's works was being dissected on the stage of an anonymous apartment, in a Rio de Janeiro neighborhood lost on the world's outskirts. Outside, the birds' singing made up a chorus.

"Our little birds . . ." the woman mentioned cheerfully. "They're quite exuberant today!"

"What's annoying is the six o'clock clanging of the church

bells on the corner," interjected the young man, in keeping with the pleasantries.

"Tell me about it," said the older man.

However, having considered several options, the writer preferred to return to the task at hand. "Mourning for a glory that can't be restored."

"True enough, true enough," his visitor hastened to affirm.

The smile that kept them going encouraged the woman to leave Italy to pay homage to a French author. "And then?" she asked.

"Then . . ." the super began, still attempting to find a way to broach the subject that had brought him there.

But changing gears and succumbing to the impetuousness of his Sicilian heritage, he continued: ". . . my favorite character is Prince Tancredi, played by Alain Delon in the film. Not the Prince of Salina . . . A lovable cynic, Tancredi is! Had the story taken place in the twentieth century, the guy would be a fascist in support of Mussolini."

He'd even managed to have the last word, the apartment dwellers thought, one savoring the fact, the other gnashing his teeth.

"Wonderful, this conversation of ours," his wife ventured to say with a sigh, "it almost feels like a dream."

And without giving her husband time to interrupt, she made room for what was to come. "Well . . . I'll leave you now. I imagine the two of you have important things to discuss."

"Yes," agreed their guest, adding with the elegance that, for better or worse, had prevailed in the room, "although your opinion would have been most welcome."

11

The couple had clearly been affected by the visit, albeit in different ways. *Irritated* perhaps described the husband's mood best. It was inconceivable, considering the ideas exchanged and valued by both men, that the guest would have had the gall to . . .

He was at a loss for words. Were he to speak his mind privately to his wife, for example, they would be unprintable.

Indeed, the visitor's mission that afternoon had evolved from delicate to thankless precisely as a result of the conversation that had preceded it. Because the young man's goal had been none other than to get on his host's good side so that his name, respected by everyone in the building, might be submitted to the condominium to . . .

. . . take over his duties as superintendent!

Confronted with the suggestion, the author had choked on his water, and from then on, he hadn't disguised his indignation at the offense committed. Shocked, he couldn't recall a single instance that had left him as baffled. Not even the fateful afternoon when one of his recent manuscripts had been rejected by his publisher.

Visconti's spirit still loomed large in their living room, surrounded by frescoes of a bygone grandeur. From that perspective, it seemed unthinkable to the writer that two such irreconcilable subjects—the beauty of a glorious era fading into nostalgia, on the one hand, and the drudgery of a modest superintendent's duties, on the other—could suddenly, and without the slightest transition, be a part of one and the same conversation.

As an artist, he felt betrayed in the deepest sense, one he deemed worthy of reverence above all else: respect for art when professed by the great masters.

Noticing how pale his host had suddenly become, the super quickly understood that he'd misstepped. Even so, he'd chosen to forge ahead. In part because he had no alternative—he needed to bring into play the reason behind his visit.

Moreover, he did not feel responsible for the verbal intrusion, into his agenda, of evocations he deemed irrelevant in light of his goals. They were, after all, merely literary figures. And characters in a film.

Proceeding with his explanations, albeit flying blindly, he claimed that, after three consecutive terms in the position, he could no longer respond to the building's needs, since he had just accepted new responsibilities at the firm where he worked. His wife and children, furthermore, complained that he didn't devote enough time to the family.

A heavy silence ensued, which the birds' chirping did little to mitigate.

If only the guest had lived up to Eva's dream, the man thought sadly. *When he'd seemed so concerned about a family on the brink of despair . . .*

Not even that, however, had happened.

"I assume that my suggestion . . ." the young man said softly, making a move to leave his seat.

"You assume correctly, my boy," interrupted the older man, getting up himself. "*One hundred percent* correctly."

As usual, it had fallen to his wife, who had come to say

good-bye when the elevator was summoned, to smooth things over. "My husband writes and therefore he's very bus—"

"You write, sir?" the young man had still had time to inquire politely.

A disaster, a true disaster . . . the husband had grumbled after verifying, through the peephole, that the elevator had departed. *Tancredi, his favorite character . . . And me, a building superintendent!*

Despite the venting, he felt depressed. He was aware that his outburst had had nothing to do with his age or a moment of weakness. And much less with the poor young man. On the contrary, it dated back to his tender childhood years—when, impatient, he had trouble expressing himself.

An ordeal, since there was no end to the information he wished to pass on to the adults around him; and his ability to do so was quite limited, whether for lack of vocabulary or due to the tremendous anxiety that left him unable to complete his tales.

As a grown man, he'd often visited a couple who had been old friends of his parents. One night, he'd listened, awed and astonished, to the two of them describe his witty remarks as a child. Awed, because he didn't remember the episodes evoked. Astonished by the enormity of what he'd assumed was buried in the ruins of his early years.

He'd felt at that time like the Phoenician poet who, at the end of his life, returned to his native village and, seeing it destroyed by a succession of wars and epidemics, didn't recognize as his own the poems of youth on parchment scrolls rediscovered amid the wreckage of his family home.

Still, he had noted on scraps of paper and the back of an envelope the details preserved by the couple. And that same night, he'd bent over them with the reverence of someone trying to piece together ancient pottery shards. He'd vaguely discerned a few scattered islands in the distance—never terra firma.

In contrast, years later, he'd blessed the hour in which he'd managed to produce a sentence with a beginning, middle, and end, although not in that order. The rest would be easy, he thought. He hardly wanted for stories to tell. But . . .

. . . *where could they have gone? If his archipelago had disappeared off the map and only the seas remained?*

12

His thoughts kept drifting back to his teen years, for a reason as romantic as it was strategic: This phase had followed closely on the heels of his early childhood—and, because of this, he nurtured the hope of regaining access to those even more distant years.

To no avail. He was stopped on the border of time, like an undocumented traveler who could hardly give his name—much less communicate the purpose of his return to those parts.

He looked over the vast expanse where so much had blossomed—a landscape that today appeared a wasteland to him. Nothing was left. His stories had vanished without a trace. As in a natural disaster.

Hybrid, like a personal cataclysm. Very similar, on the infinitesimal level of the individual, to a large-scale tremor of the Earth's crust, which, rather than creating rifts or mountains, opening seas and separating continents, obliterated his past. Hadn't the dinosaurs disappeared in seconds thanks to an asteroid from outer space? Something far simpler had happened in the case of his tiny anomaly. Something that would never be visible to the naked eye. He therefore had no way of arriving at his personal mine of ideas—regardless of its size and depth. The link had simply broken. The passionate child had given way to the restless youth, who merely felt nostalgic for who he had been. A feeling that, on the brink of adulthood, was not in the least bit tragic, but rather pathetic.

Without a second thought, he replaced ideas with ideals. And participated in all the protest movements of his generation. During one of them, spraying graffiti on walls, he'd met his wife. Together, they'd agreed the world needed to be set on fire. They lived through May 1968 and dedicated themselves to the cause with passion. They'd been imprisoned. But the pendulum swung, and they'd ended up being released a few days later. In the early days of the repression, small miracles took place every so often, which led the young to behave like naïve heroes.

At the same time, he'd reinvented himself—with promising results. But the many changes of plans over the next twenty years wore him out. Like an animal fleeing a devastating fire deep in the forest, he veered off on the wrong trails without missing a beat, advancing along sinuous paths, unaware they were detours.

13

Rereading was more important than reading, as the truths were hidden between the lines. And these ended up incorporating variants that infiltrated the text even further—until they vanished. Which complicated the search, overwhelming his memory.

He found himself with no appetite for labyrinths. Thus, he regarded his text the way, fifty years earlier, he had contemplated his smooth white wall in a back alley of his neighborhood moments before hearing the distressed voice say, "Any black paint left in your can, comrade?"

Comrade . . . And wearing a beret à la Che Guevara on top of that . . .

"Nope, just red," he'd replied promptly. But he'd added lightly, "Pessimism rules. We're out of black."

She'd laughed and said in the same tone, "That's how Mondays are. The black gets used up over the weekend. Haven't you noticed?"

The young woman seemed to speak from experience.

"No . . . It's my first time."

"How's that, comrade? First time against the *paredón?*"

"You never forget your first."

They'd kept the banter going, trading smiles and furtive glances that scarcely contained their mutual delight. And that night, after catching a Woody Allen film, they'd crossed the street and grabbed a bite at Beco da Fome with a filmmaker friend of his. The three stood, jostling for a place at the counter with cabdrivers and hippies.

Eva had been impressed with the filmmaker and he with her, since she'd revealed having seen one of his films at the local Museum of Modern Art, in a crowd of eight, which had included the artist's parents.

Looking at the two, he'd realized that if he blundered, he'd lose the young woman then and there. He took a deep breath and whispered in her ear, "How many sticks would make a good canoe? Do you know?"

"*What?*" she asked, momentarily shifting her attention away from the filmmaker.

"Never mind. What are you doing tomorrow?"

"Spray-painting buildings. Going to the movies. And grabbing a bite with you, sweetheart."

The filmmaker left shortly afterward. Passing by his friend, he murmured, "Go for it."

He had. For fifty years.

14

Both had grown up as only children—but in different ways. That was what had brought them together. In a matter of days, they became inseparable. And whereas his parents, who were living abroad, knew little of his involvement with the young woman, hers were present and doted on him as he hadn't been as a child. Years later, in times of crisis, when he and Eva considered separating, the impossibility of severing ties with his in-laws weighed as heavily as parting with his wife.

When, in 2010 or 2011, a popular women's magazine had included a feature on couples "who had been through everything together," the two had avoided discussing the secret to their accomplishment, conceding that they had no way of really knowing. ("Who cares?" Eva had asked, while he'd promised to check with his wife's cats, "who had strong opinions on the matter.")

They had, however, agreed on one noteworthy point: They were different enough to have remained interested in each other. They were both artists, she a photographer (later a journalist), he a pianist (later a writer). And if, at first, their personal disagreements had been cause for concern, their fast-paced work lives smoothed these over, revealing them for what they were: a constant source of surprise.

That was the most they were willing to acknowledge: life

as a set of building blocks. The kind that fascinate children—when they have access to them at the right age. "A blindfolded race," he'd added, before continuing with the analogy, "a puzzle in which certain pieces are left out . . ."

The reporter had jotted down the words, which ended up serving as the title and subtitle of her article: "Building Blocks: When Certain Pieces Are Left Out."

After the interview, they'd shared a nice relaxed moment. Poring over the photos and series of articles published by Eva in newspapers and magazines over the course of her career, the reporter had pulled out an old photo of an elderly couple sitting on a park bench and asked, "And what about this image?"

"It's us," Eva had replied, while her husband laughed softly.

"The two of you?"

After studying the forty-year-old photo more closely, the reporter had hesitated. "But . . ."

"It's us *today,*" Eva had insisted, closing the box of old articles and then asking, "Coffee, anyone?"

"Don't worry," the husband had whispered in the young reporter's ear. "In my stories, she's always offering water or coffee at the most unlikely times."

15

One afternoon, he'd again sought refuge in the past, and had opened a heavy trunk in which assorted letters and records fought for space with old manuscripts. Among the collected memories, he had flipped through the pages of a few photo albums.

One image in particular held his attention. His parents appeared in it, side by side and in profile, at some diplomatic reception, he in a dark suit, with a tumbler of whiskey in hand and a slight smile, she in a light dress, on the brink of smiling.

Had the photo been taken a moment later, she would have smiled. But there would always have been the risk that, in that second image, his father would have remained serious. The social choreographies to which they were subject made way for counterpoints.

Anyhow, in that photo his mother was simply looking. At what? Not at those present. She was looking beyond them. Or, perhaps even more absent, through them.

In the photo, his parents were almost twenty-five years *younger* than he was now. Seen in perspective, the difference didn't mean much, since it reflected nothing but numbers; but from another angle—the one that mattered—the fact moved him as it brought to light losses and divergences that had stitched together or frayed their fate, weaving a tapestry that had been a part of his heritage ever since.

A tapestry that would be passed along one day, with the weight of the varied herds that had trod on it, coming and going, hesitating and plodding onward, leaving embedded—among threads, seams, patches, and fibers—outlines of the countless stories he had inherited.

Stories interwoven with dreams and nightmares he had no control over, either—the images surprised him constantly, sometimes even stunned him. Had his father threatened to throw his mother overboard in the middle of the Mediterranean one stormy night? Or had he merely raised his voice at her over dessert in the luxury vessel's first-class dining room, in a tone that the child, in his high chair, had found intimidating? Leading him to bring the threatening sound back to his cabin berth and, later, merge it with the dark waves beneath which his mother had disappeared—to resurface, dry as could be, hair neatly done, and all smiles, the next morning?

The photograph he now held hadn't caught his attention until then, perhaps because it was smaller than the others, or because it wasn't in an album, probably having slipped out of one of them, or from some envelope. But upon studying it closely, he'd discovered, to his surprise, that he, too, appeared in the image—only partially cut off. (On the pad beside his laptop, he noted in pencil, "Suggest to publisher as book cover.")

The part that was missing was his right side. But there was no doubt that it was him (and not some other half person); he recognized the profile he'd flaunted in his youth, from the well-combed hair and the slim silhouette, which he'd gradually lose over the years. It didn't matter that none of his face, not even an eye, could be seen. And that only the left ear had survived.

It was half of him.

Him, the way he was used to being seen by his parents, uttering unfinished statements, or beginning a story midway through. Because since childhood he'd thought more than he spoke. (As such, when he opened his mouth, he plowed ahead; or, if he closed it, he did so too soon. And if, as a child, he'd been appreciated for his prolific illogical conclusions, in his teen years, he'd paid the price.)

While still a young boy, he had been taken to a psychologist to address the problem. Just before wrapping up the consultation, the doctor had asked to spend a moment alone with him. How old could he have been at the time? Four? Five? The fact is that after a few minutes the therapist had taken him back out to his parents. And, upon opening the exit door, the doctor had held himself back, merely looking at the two adults with an expression of heavy sadness.

His mother always recounted this episode with a somewhat nervous laugh, as if she felt the doctor had exaggerated—in judging them so harshly. And he'd never been able to find out if the scene had happened as his mother described it; or if, momentarily feeling wicked, his mother had revised the vignette, which could be taken as true and, therefore, join the framed pictures he sometimes availed himself of in mounting his imaginary exhibitions. ("That portrait, the third from the right, is from his dark blue period," some visitor glancing through a possible catalog might remark, before adding, in a lower voice that few would hear, since he couldn't be sure that those words had actually been spoken, "the period after the electroshocks.")

He noted that, in the photo, he stood three feet or so behind his parents. As if a discreet line had been drawn that left him neither close to nor far from them. He was where he'd always been: halfway between two impossibilities. And that's what was impressive—the position's coherence.

Just whom it impressed, however, he didn't know. Because the world remained indifferent.

It was, nonetheless, a coherence that hovered around the child, like a refuge permanently available to him—enabling the boy a grounding cable to set on land whenever he wished. Something that the photographer had captured so well simply by chance.

Thus, perhaps, the sadness of his childhood doctor, whose look had conveyed the same helplessness we sometimes feel when close to solving great mysteries—which elude us owing to the capricious behavior of others. The doctor had managed to see the child on the verge of something. Of what didn't matter. Only that he had been on the verge. Just as his wife, in her dream, had seen the little girl. She, too, on the verge of something.

Before closing the trunk, it dawned on him that an eternity separated the image in his hands from the apartment where he now found himself with his wife, on a day that, like so many others, had started out sunny and ended up gray—their routines as shut-ins lulling them into a lethargic numbness, from which they both emerged only at night, to watch the news on TV in silence.

Distracted as always, he had at some point stuck two fingers into his shirt pocket to see what it held—a candy, a loose button, an aspirin?—only to come across the photo again. At that moment, following on the TV screen a trailer for a documentary about the nineteenth-century Napoleonic campaigns, he'd asked himself, *Where might my other half be today?*

16

For a while, he continued to think about his other half, whom he named M. And, without realizing it, he began to talk to him.

Although the duality intrigued him at first, he couldn't deny that the voice was *his*, as were the thoughts that came and went in that clandestine frequency. Not even the fact that the illusion occasionally imposed itself on reality kept him from ignoring the evidence.

The phenomenon hadn't ever threatened his self-confidence—in the sense of upsetting him. The exchanges between the two reminded him of the Bach fugues that he'd played in his youth. In which, immediately after the first notes, he'd forget who was in charge of the melodic line—the right hand, which had started it, or the left, reacting to it—thereby opening space for the succession of flourishes and designs that in the end blended together seamlessly. And if the analogy was imperfect, like any that dared to compare word and melody, it nevertheless helped to suggest the agility, coherence, and intimacy with which the fragments of phrases reached his ears.

These displays occurred at any time, and in every way were reminiscent of the reveries and fantasies of Norse mythology. Except that there was nothing lyrical or introspective about the exercise evoked here, all of it owing, on the contrary, to something much more prosaic and playful.

In this case, to a simple game of Ping-Pong, in which the little ball took on the role of ideas. And the comparison wasn't altogether far-fetched, in that the dialogues were often fun. As if they were a game. And why not? After all, he'd reached an age when, just like a certain celebrated poet, he considered himself to contain multitudes. He and M had lived through so many situations that the crossroads produced along the way ended up seeming normal.

He usually stuck to this more pedestrian interpretation of the game between them, and marveled at the speed and allure of the back-and-forth he was a part of. The lines came and went, without the invisible net over the table creating an obstacle.

Inevitably, Eva began to catch him talking to himself in the hallway. This was not exactly news. But what she heard worried her.

17

"Insanity, M?"

And why not?

"The suggestion that we're sliding toward the unknown . . ."

. . . is revealing, nonetheless.

"Of something greater?"

Most likely.

"Who knows . . ."

That doesn't scare me.

"But it worries Eva. . . ."

I actually find it tempting.

"Eva on the one hand, you on the other."

Me? But if I don't even exist . . .

"You meddle; therefore you exist."

It's my sacred right: to avoid . . .

". . . the screens."

Put up to justify the fluctuations of your story.

"Like Eva's walls . . ."

Setting fire to her gunpowder magazine.

"A powerful image, isn't it?"

Is it? Few know what a gunpowder magazine is.

"Incensed, the rebellious soldiers set fire to their gunpowder magazine."

What we need . . .
". . . is to set fire . . ."
. . . to our magazine.

18

He no longer recalled exactly when M had begun to complicate his life. Such was the fate of certain daydreams, he supposed, when they take us by surprise—and eventually consume us. He would, at times, have liked to keep his partner at a distance. Unable to do so, he had tried to avoid him.

But all in due time, as his grandmother would have advised. He had always appreciated her pearls of wisdom. "Better safe than sorry," the poor dear used to say, trembling with fear whenever he gave her a lift in his little convertible. Rightfully so. He drove with the reckless abandon that the young mistake for sophistication and savoir faire. Left hand on the steering wheel, the right anywhere but toward their destination (in the glove compartment in search of a cassette, in his pocket in search of a cigarette), the yellow light ahead signaling an invitation. How could he resist?

He'd accelerate the car and, conversely, decelerate his text (as M, who now rode alongside them, would have put it). Let's say he might be taking a break from his manuscript and head up Avenida Atlântica with his grandmother on a sunny Sunday to drop her off at some corner of Copacabana, where, with a colorful dress, hat, and handbag, she'd be meeting a friend.

Extraordinary to think that, today, he was the exact same age his grandmother had been then. Thus the wish to embrace the dear old woman and ask her all sorts of questions about the past.

His old trunk was too small to hold answers to the inquiries he'd never made—of her and of his parents. Inquiries that, every now and then, he'd revisited with deep regret.

It would have been interesting if, at age four, he'd had the means to tug his father's sleeve and try to remove the doubt that, for years, had kept him awake at night. "Daddy, that night on the ship, did you really want to throw Mommy overboard?"

Not that this was the question that mattered most, especially since he'd never dismissed the notion that he'd dreamed the scene. More appropriate, perhaps, and still related to the topic, would have been to shift the emphasis and catch his mother's attention with something pertinent: "Mommy, why did I *dream* that Daddy threw you overboard?"

Better . . . Because his mother read a lot, more than his father, and might allude to Jung or Freud in search of some explanation that would put her son's mind at ease—or alarm him even further.

In all likelihood, she would have turned the page of the novel she was reading, patted him gently on the head, and sent him back to his room.

"Go on, my boy. Go play."

Thus avoiding the question that would barely have reached her ears; or which, having gotten through to her—and been answered—would have forced her son to face issues so complex that not even regurgitated would they have been digested and permeated his soul.

He didn't remember at what age he'd begun to bite his

nails, a habit he'd never managed to give up but that now seemed well worth investigating.

"Daddy, can't you see that we're caught in a vicious circle, where I bite my nails because you spank me and you spank me because I bite my nails?"

19

Regurgitated? Permeating your soul?

"Yes, M. It's when the gastric content of the stomach . . ."

I know what regurgitated *means!*

"So?"

So, I don't know what that gem is doing in your text! Along with so many others!

"My texts aren't spaces seeking acceptance. Or worthy of attention."

Nineteenth-century carriages, Napoleonic wars, punctured canoes, dinner gongs . . .

"Don't go there, M. . . ."

. . . hay bales that complain . . .

"Okay. Cool it."

. . . lumberjacks dragging women on moonlit nights . . .

"C'mon now . . ."

In a chaotic world like ours, riddled with tragedies and injustices . . .

"For the love of . . ."

. . . not to mention the climate crisis, the collapse of biodiversity . . .

"All crucial topics, I agree, M . . ."

. . . hatred being spread around the world, racism, geopolitical tensions . . .

"But it's also important to be open to . . ."

. . . a Phoenician poet! A Phoenician poet!

"One of my stranger characters, I admit, but nevertheless . . ."

. . . a tube of toothpaste!

"One way, like any other, of . . ."

Getting somewhere?

"Of concentrating on *what interests me.* On fleeting existences."

Fleeting existences? Where did you get that from?

"Advice Baudelaire gave Edouard Manet."

Meaning . . .

". . . not to paint the obvious, M. *Not* to paint the obvious."

Quite curious, your collection of fleeting existences: a building super, a steward . . .

". . . fleeting but *relevant.* Each in its own way. Like my Phoenician po—"

. . . a coachman, a psychic, a lumberjack, the walls of Jericho . . .

"Every era has its baggage. Invisible though it may be . . ."

What about ours? Our personal baggage?

"We'll get to that, M. We won't venture off without it."

20

M interfered in his work more and more often. In so doing, he forgot the respect warranted by basic social norms, not to mention rules of etiquette—especially as a guest, as was the case here, in someone else's head.

As for our author, he remained faithful to the principle of clinging ferociously to his opening sentence as the seed of his text. A line born untethered, free of assumptions or expectations. Without obligations. Among them, the most insidious of all: getting somewhere.

A sentence that required room to breathe and look around. Never demands that would tie it to a fate. *A sentence that needed to feel at ease.* To sow and be sown.

In this phase of creation, it reigned supreme, over the page—and over *him.* Not because the future was uncertain; that hardly mattered! *But because of the role it had played until that very moment.* It was quite possible that, at some later stage, buried beneath subsequent drafts, the sentence would disappear without a trace. Yet its importance would not be diminished—it would have served its purpose. And the text, albeit motherless, would never be an orphan.

He, too, was willing to make this supreme sacrifice on the personal level. Once the language had been discovered, and access to its mysteries secured, he, as writer, didn't mind exiting the scene, going the way of his rough drafts. What mattered was the work, never some vague authorship bound to be forgotten.

M disagreed with his comments, when he didn't outright laugh at them. He had even compared one of his chapters to a thoroughbred horse (*Arabian,* he'd actually specified) that galloped through fields of green for a while but, having gradually lost its noble standing, would ultimately take on the appearance of an old nag hobbling through a desolate landscape. M had attributed this to the author's indulgence with the text, as well as to its lack of an anchor that would assure the chapter at least some consistency on the journey from start to finish.

He couldn't imagine where M had come up with his Arabian horse. But he knew that this perspective reflected faulty vision on his companion's part. And he was quite prepared to admit that M was right—if getting somewhere was, in fact, the aim of a text.

But what if its raison d'être was to drift between the lines, perhaps rooting around among the words—without fear of open spaces?

Dissecting the infinite possibilities of a simple tube of toothpaste, for example? Squeezing it to death and then studying it? To land at an inn lost somewhere on the European continent on the cusp of the nineteenth century?

For him, the sentence was bait; for M, the fish.

The mystery of M's sentence was over precisely when he pondered the page and wrote down four letters. F-i-s-h. End of mystery.

The mystery of his own sentence didn't begin even when the bait surfaced. Because, albeit rooted in the real world, his bait wasn't the kind cast into the water at the end of a hook. At most it could be mistaken for the shadows of the leaves that would dance at night on his bedroom ceiling, pointing the direction his manuscripts should take.

He'd resisted debating the issue to avoid annoying M. But if it had gone further, he would've added that his sentence—the first of any manuscript of his—was no more than an innocent invitation. Because it didn't know the nature, relevance, or content of the ideas lying in wait.

It was up to them to catch the sentence. Not the other way around.

He'd often imagined that, somewhere in the universe, there was a living archive of ideas available to whoever wished to gather them, just as, in the real world, a rich data bank existed for anyone who sought to consult it.

If one of his characters had described life as a set of building blocks, reminding us that sometimes pieces didn't fit together, he wanted to have the freedom to agree. Eventually, however, he would also have liked to suggest a different view, according to which life could take on the form of an endless canvas, where fiction and reality merged with the inconsistency of dreams.

21

One afternoon, as inevitably happens in certain situations, they sat down on the living room sofa for a chat. It was Eva's turn to put forward her sentence.

"My mother always used to say that *there are none so blind as those who will not see.*"

He waited. It wasn't by chance that they'd lived together for so many years. He recalled an expression that his own mother often used—and thought to himself that he and Eva *knew each other inside out.* He realized that, with her remark, Eva had offered him the opportunity to step into the scene under the cover of a simple aphorism.

It just so happens, though, that *hasty decisions*—as his grandmother would've said—*didn't always lead to the best outcomes.*

He then understood that they had been joined by three women, one of them from two generations ago. Three women whose wisdom owed a great deal to myriad simple truths usually hidden from view.

So he focused on two objective details. If an old-fashioned duel was about to take place, the sort that relied on pistols or swords, Eva would need a couple of witnesses—since his mother and grandmother wouldn't hesitate to serve as his seconds. As for the setting, he further considered, the living room would need to give way to a woodside garden, where the encounter would occur on the dewy grass of the early-morning hours. For that was the usual backdrop of the sixteenth-century duels that had set the precious adventure books of his childhood on fire.

It was the sound of the birds congregating at twilight that brought him back to his living room, the languid look of which soothed him, to the degree that he almost missed his wife's cats. Nothing in those surroundings evoked struggles or duels. Depending on how things went, there was little in that familiar landscape of theirs that could be associated with stress or drama.

Drawing out the pause that had followed Eva's comment wasn't a good idea, though. Even if the silence was intended to remove the apprehension that had momentarily come between the two of them.

He decided to go back to the blind man who still waited in their living room. But he chose to do so as succinctly as possible.

"And . . .?"

She took up the challenge quite naturally and went even further, leaving a lag time between her words.

"And you . . ."

The walls of Jericho slowly began to implode. He felt that, in a matter of seconds, he would be buried beneath a mix of earth, clay, rocks, and . . .

". . . go around talking to yourself in the hallways."

Saved by the gong.

"But that's what I do when I'm writing." He smiled quickly. "When I'm working on my dialogues. I don't even remember how many times you've called for my atten—"

"Except that, quite often . . ." she said, holding up her hand, a gesture she rarely resorted to.

"Quite often . . ."

"... what you say doesn't make any sense."

Doesn't make any sense?

He had no way to parry the blow. And it was intended as a blow, of that he was certain. So much so that the witnesses had shuddered. (Or so he thought.) A low, almost disloyal blow, since the comment had transported him straight back to the dyslexia of his youth. There was nothing to do but take a deep breath.

And try to make a joke of it.

"Have you finally figured out how many sticks would go into that infamous canoe of ours?" he asked, raising his bushy eyebrows.

She understood. Beyond the kidding, so often repeated, she understood the fear. And conceded, with a brief tender look, that perhaps she had gone too far. At the same time, he, as husband, suddenly became aware of the extent of his wife's concern.

"Is it really that ... *strange?*" he asked softly.

The witnesses gathered up the weapons from the field and exited the scene.

It was her turn to smile.

"Not really," she said, feeling his discomfort, "but it's curious. Because I can't figure out what you're saying."

Here, Eva hesitated, and he, resigned, knew to wait once more.

"I don't recognize the *language*. It's ..."

They'd arrived at what, in his story, he was in the habit of calling no-man's-land.

Who better than her to accompany him on the journey?

"It's unrecognizable. It seems unintelligible."

And who better than him to know that?

She held off for a few seconds, as if trying to remember something.

"And when I do recognize it, it's beyond comprehension."

"It's beyond comprehension?"

"'Me? A super!' you grumbled one time. 'And Tancredi, his favorite character!'"

Once again, the gong had come to his rescue. This time categorically, unmistakably.

"Of course . . . It was right after Luiz Bernardo left here."

"Who?"

"The super! Our super! When Luiz Bernardo came to see us . . ."

"Luiz Bernardo never came up here."

"Yes, days after you dreamed about him, remember?"

"Me? *I dreamed about our super?*"

Again his desolate landscape. Again the swamp. With each step, he sank a bit more.

22

"Are you comfortable? Seat belt not too tight?"

"No . . . I'm fine. The seat is comfortable. And you?"

"All's okay with me."

"Could we ask the driver to go slowly?"

"He knows, he knows . . ."

"My wife is going to try to follow us."

"The driver is aware. Your wife spoke with him."

"She's bringing my things in our car."

"I know. I helped carry your bag down."

"That's right. Thank you."

"There's no traffic at this hour, so no rush."

"Do you like your job? Taking people from here to there?"

"Very much. It varies a lot. No two days are alike. . . ."

"I like my work, too."

"Yeah? What do you do?"

"I also take people from here to there."

"You don't say!"

"Give me a sentence and I'll move the Earth!"

"Come again?"

"Archimedes. The point of support."

"Archi—"

"—medes. A Greek philosopher. The Archimedean point of support is all it takes. For the lever."

"For the lever?"

"Yes . . . that's what I came up with."

"You came up with the lever?"

"No. I came up with the sentence. That's what gives the story its leverage."

"Nice!"

"Isn't it? *But the sentence is always at risk.* They could take it away."

"The way they steal everything in this country . . ."

"Exactly, *exactly, my friend* . . . Do you write, too?"

"Do I *write?* Sure, I write. I mean, I know *how* to wri—"

"Do your sentences have a beginning, middle, and end?"

"Beginning, middle, and . . ."

"Yes. In that order or any other."

"I write down addresses. And sometimes I take notes."

"Notes are important. I keep a pad at hand just for them. Come to think of it . . ."

"What?"

"I forgot my pad at home! Do you think we could go ba—?"

"What do you write about?"

"Stories. Big, green, thin, tall . . ."

"Really?"

". . . small, purple, fat, short . . ."

"That's great . . ."

"It's not always easy."

"I can imagine! But where do they come from . . . where do the . . ."

"Words come from? Depends. This ambulance."

"This ambulance?"

"All you have to do is stay alert. Comfortably seated. And in silence."

"In the middle of traffic? With people honk—"

"What happens out there doesn't matter. Only in here."

"Only in . . ."

"Yes. Here between us."

"Between us . . ."

"In complete silence."

"Can't we speak softly?

"Sure. Softly is okay. What matters . . ."

"What matters . . ."

". . . is the sentence."

"The sentence."

"Yes. And then, after it . . ."

"After it . . ."

". . . the editing."

"Ah . . ."

"From then on, you just take a deep breath and . . . and . . ."

"Is your seat belt bothering you?"

"No. I just wanted to be sure that my wife is indeed behind us."

"The green car?"

"I can't turn around on account of this seat—"

"The car is right behind us. You can relax. I'm keeping an eye out."

"Thanks a lot."

"*What happens out there doesn't matter. . . .*"

"Exactly . . . You catch on quickly!"

"You're a good teacher. And what comes next?"

"Next? The secret."

"The secret?"

"Finding the way to . . . *get into someone else's head.*"

"Imagine that!

"Through the back door. Never through the front door. But *not* to tell something."

"No?"

"No . . . Telling something is easy. *But leaving an impression* . . . Something that stays."

"Something that stays. In the other person's head?"

"You've got it. Right in there. Deep in the person's head."

"That stays with that person . . ."

". . . from here to there. And from there to here. Like the two of us, going through this tunnel."

"It makes sense. *Makes perfect sense.*"

"Right?"

"Right. Except . . . If you'll forgive my . . ."

"Yes?"

" . . . *forgive my question* . . ."

"Ask away, my friend."

"You're going to be admitted, aren't you? To the hospital?"

"The psych ward? Yes, I am. And for a while there, you were under the impression that . . ."

"Precisely . . ."

"Get it?"

Part III

23

"Good morning."

"Good morning, Doctor."

The sessions always started with this exchange. Words they each uttered in the same tone, between cautious and optimistic. With a smile, he took leave of the nurse who had helped him to the armchair facing the psychiatrist. And who would return for him later.

The ritual didn't bother him; he knew that *something* would happen during the session. When a few steps would be taken on a journey he considered pointless, although not entirely devoid of merit. As far as he was concerned, however, there would be countless forks in the road ahead and few shortcuts.

The weariness of the first few days had worn off. And with it the qualms he'd felt getting out of the ambulance. The transition from fiction to reality had been rather abrupt. At home, it was usually smooth, so that he barely noticed it. But suddenly . . .

Suddenly, a new world. That his wife wouldn't be a part of. Which had left him anxious at first—hindering his ability to deal with the challenge. They'd both entered uncharted territory, as unfamiliar to his eyes as to Eva's. Except that her perspective was that of a visitor. Whereas his was of one who stayed. At night, that made a difference.

Less so by day. The environment actually seemed designed for him. *Custom-made* might have been the right term—like a suit cut by a tailor who'd sized him up with a glance or two. Various routines completed the outfit: the regularly scheduled mealtimes, the bathing, the group activities. And the dispensing of medicine. All that was missing was the open door so that *someone might enter.* Of all the patients, only he seemed to have noticed its nonexistence.

His room, on the ground floor, had just one window. But it looked out at a tree, planted in the middle of the courtyard. At certain times of day, he was allowed free time in the garden.

His new surroundings . . . There would be other birds. But since the neighborhoods weren't far apart, some of his sparrows might visit him. He'd noted there were bars on the second-floor windows, disguised as trellises. Whom would they fool?

Back at the apartment, Eva had emerged out of nowhere and, crossing her arms, planted herself with her back to the window. She'd blocked the way with her gaze. It hadn't been an imposition. Nor a plea. At most, it was kindness.

Par delicatesse / J'ai perdu ma vie . . .

And now, he saw himself obliged to face the entanglement of those morning sessions.

Do you like French poetry, Doctor? From the nineteenth century?

A man between fifty and sixty. Facing the Parthenon. Not knowing what to make of those ruins. Sending him back to his room after an innocuous exchange, without so much as a pat on the head.

Go on, my boy. Go play.

Behind the desk, the doctor consulted a notebook. A methodical, organized professional.

He felt at a disadvantage—his notepad had been forgotten

at home. At his request, Eva had read over the phone the last observation he'd jotted down: "Suggest to publisher as book cover."

He had no idea what those words meant.

24

The psychiatrist had asked Eva about the window. Where she'd gotten her impression—that her husband would jump.

"It wasn't an impression," she had replied, correcting him quite emphatically. "A certainty."

Then she'd softened her tone. "He'd been confused for a while. But he seemed sad. A profound sadness brought on by I don't know what . . ."

The doctor chose to reassure her. "Your husband seems better here. And he's responding well to treatment. He likes our garden and spends hours sitting on a bench under a tree near his room. Sometimes he reads, but not always. The hospital has a decent library; a lot of books are donated by families after the patients . . ."

A moment of hesitation.

". . . are discharged," Eva said.

They were facing each other, Eva in the same chair her husband had sat in that morning. "With his *imaginary scale,*" the psychiatrist had said, quoting the patient.

Language that, according to him, he'd gradually managed to unravel. On one hand, *everything that had come before*. On the other, *the enormity of what was yet to come*. And between the two—always in the patient's words—*time, the only variable that could be counted on*.

"I like the idea," he'd added. "Time as the balancing scale. When, as we well know, time isn't exactly relia—"

"Do you think he's going to be all right?"

The doctor had preferred to fend off the question. Especially because, as of yet, he had no basis for comparisons of any kind.

He casually informed her, "Your husband shows no signs of self-destructive behavior. Far from it. Despite having mentioned that, when he was four—"

"I've never believed in that supposed childhood suicide attempt. That prank with the jar of vitamins . . . Not even his sister, who finds the story hilarious, believes it."

"He has a sister?"

"And a younger brother."

"The books . . ."

They'd finally gotten to what mattered. Midway between the childhood depression and the author's stubbornness. Ground they could cover without fear.

"He told me he's published several books," the doctor continued. "He even gave me one of them."

He stood and went to the bookcase, returning with the copy in hand.

"I haven't read it yet. But he told me that, after the fourth novel, he gave up everything to write. And that, for thirty years, he hasn't done anything else. He's written several other books."

"Several other manuscripts."

"Manuscripts?"

She nodded and said, "He hasn't let a day go by without writing. As if he lived through his characters. He did translations to make ends meet. They were well received."

"Exactly how many . . ."

". . . *manuscripts?* I lost count. They were a lot, over the course of thirty years."

"None of them published?"

She paused briefly.

"One at our own expense. The others were all rejected by the publishers. But that didn't deter him, or even discourage him. He kept writing, as if it didn't matter."

The doctor pushed ahead. "Your husband spoke of editions published abroad. He mentioned a conversation between his agent and a German publisher."

"Poetic license . . . The European editions, the agent, the German publisher . . . Freud's great-grandson at that! What he says gets mixed up with what he writes. . . . And what he writes rarely has to do with real life. His, at least."

Reshelving the book in his hand, the doctor asked, "And the four books that were published?"

"Riveting, all of them. Each in its own way. But they went unnoticed. The reviews, at the time of their release, were modest or lackluster. In some cases, almost nonexistent. No one remembers them today."

She smiled in a show of solidarity.

"I was worried. He wasn't. Over time . . ."

"Over time . . ."

". . . I started to sense that he was moving back and forth between fiction and reality with surprising agility. As if he'd created a kind of game for himself. He dreamed up fictitious interviews, university lectures, correspondence with enthusiastic readers. . . . At first, I found it entertaining. But, over time, I saw that he no longer distinguished between the two. . . . The truth is that he never second-guessed his talent."

"That couldn't have been . . ."

". . . *easy?* For me? It was never easy."

The doctor suddenly craved the cigarettes he'd given up ten years earlier.

"It was ... *different.* Among other reasons because I was upgraded from wife to character. Without ever ceasing to be a reader ... and editor."

Here she laughed. The doctor, in turn, realized what had kept the couple together for so many years.

"Our life was magical. . . ."

And to herself: *Is magical.*

25

To his surprise, things weren't that bad in his new surroundings. Mostly because going back to the past and to his childhood—a constant theme over the course of his life as either an obstacle or an obsession—had yielded to the novelty represented by his room and the single tree. In a matter of days, his imagination had fallen prey to the charms of both.

If probed by others—the doctor, for example, or his wife on one of her visits—he wouldn't know how to explain. The room was spacious but ordinary; and nothing set the tree apart from all the others he had been fond of. Yet there was something pleasant and dreamlike *in the combination of those two settings*, the impact of which he couldn't quite pinpoint. If required, he would define their effects: *Both were soothing places*. Had they been loaded with memories, none of them would have had anything to do with him. Unlike the apartment where he had lived for more than fifty years, where no wall or baseboard ever missed the chance to strike up a conversation with him.

He didn't sense time passing. He let himself drift, immersed in the pleasure.

With pleasure came surrender. The doctor had attributed the change, in part, to the medication he was being given. His wife, in turn, had alluded to the sense of freedom, which had led her husband to breathe out in the the garden—in contrast to the confinement they'd both been subjected to for months on end.

Without being mistaken, they were both somewhat off. For they found themselves miles from his small oasis and had no way of getting closer. States of mind, only in no-man's-land.

Well-being ... A feeling similar to what he experienced when he wrote. *Except that he was no longer writing.* He'd freed himself of the burden, of the self-serving need that he'd always felt. To photograph, make music, review films, write novels, plant trees, be the life of the party or king of the mountain ... He'd left the stage to those with greater needs, parting ways with basically absent audiences.

It didn't matter how many years of life he had left. In his last manuscript, he'd taken down a line from the closing scene of one of his favorite films, in which, at the peak of the Renaissance and the height of his scaffolding, a disciple of Giotto asks himself, while he paints the frescoes of Santa Chiara's monastery, "Why carry out a work of art when it is so much sweeter to dream about it?"

Time had vanished for him and, with it, anxiety.

26

Of all the spaces he'd come to know during this new phase, the only one that still intrigued him, on account of its apparent strangeness, was the dining room. First impressions tending to last, he hadn't yet shed the ones that had stayed with him since the day of his arrival. For it had been at the entrance to that large room, which had looked quite full to him—when he'd toured the premises with Eva and the director—that the idea of *joining a larger community of people* had first dawned on him. Until then, they'd passed by only small groups in the corridors, in the library, and in the garden.

To complicate things further, all heads had turned upon seeing them stopped in the doorway. It was inevitable that he, more so than Eva or the director, would have felt inspected. As if, by his mere presence, he personified a novelty. Could it be that, after so many years, he had finally found his public?

Either way, he'd sensed nothing hostile in the collective gaze that had lingered on his person for a moment. Time enough for him to make a mental note of the ten tables, nearly all occupied by four people, plus six smaller ones, with two seats each, alongside the windows. Were the grass outside replaced by the sea, he'd again be aboard one of the luxury cruise ships of his childhood.

"This is where we have our meals," the director had casually remarked.

But the reason he'd remained intrigued by that space also had to do with the scene he'd come upon that very afternoon, when it had been converted into a cafe by means of three Chinese screens, all decorated with golden dragons against a red background, judiciously positioned along the length of the room—thereby creating a special intimacy around the tables. And this pleased him, given his familiarity with literary screens. He had decided then that as soon as Eva left, his social debut would take place in that venue, which seemed quite receptive to Chinese dragons and who knew what else.

He'd headed there after unpacking his bag and putting away his belongings. When, again accompanied by the director, he'd taken leave of Eva at the exit. And begun his new life.

Sixty years had passed since, at the age of fourteen, he'd arrived in Rio de Janeiro and been taken by his parents to his new school—where he'd completed his secondary school education. Up to that point, he hadn't spent more than two years in any one country or home.

Based on these recollections, he jokingly asked himself whether he could count on having another fourteen years ahead of him. A period that would transform the eternity lived in the same apartment—first with his parents, then with Eva—into giant parentheses between these two symmetrical time frames of his existence.

Those were his thoughts as he entered the cafe and came upon the Chinese screens. It was around 4:00 P.M. and few tables were still occupied. The director, who'd taken him over to one of them (where two men close to his age and a younger woman were seated), greeted everyone, and handled the introductions. And, still deep in his thoughts, our newcomer had murmured "*Enchanté*" to each of them. None of the three men, including the director, had noticed. But the woman, sitting to his right, had leaned toward him and said softly, "*Soyez le bienvenu, cher monsieur.*"

How friendly, he'd thought. And he'd whispered back, "*Merci, chère madame,*" taking care to smile at the men, who kept watching him closely.

An environment just like any other, when it came down to it. Like many he'd come across elsewhere. And that, albeit with some effort, had made an uninhibited man of him. To the degree that he'd even played piano in public. And grown accustomed to taking part in casual conversation from which he extracted all kinds of information, including when and where to get the best cup of coffee. Then and there—as he found out—but not past 4:30, "because after that it was watered down." An observation that, added to the subtle references to nighttime medications, had been received with smiles by all.

Over the half hour that followed, he'd listened more than spoken, not without formulating a few questions of his own, however. Among them, one having to do with the screens and their provenance.

The men had no opinion on the matter. It was the woman, once again, who'd shared his affinity. And she'd done so in a pertinent way, creating an analogy with the books donated to the library to suggest—quite reasonably, in his opinion—that the screens might also have been a donation. "Especially since," as she'd added, "they do not match the rest of the furniture."

It made sense, he'd thought, sipping his coffee—which he deemed excellent, to everyone's satisfaction.

27

"Good morning."

"Good morning, Doctor."

"*Life as a set of building blocks.*"

. . .

"Something wrong with your seat?"

"No. Not with my seat."

"Surprised?"

"No. Not *surprised,* either. Not in the bad sense. It's just that . . ."

. . .

"I'm not used to being quoted. Like that. After so many years of . . ."

"My apologies! I didn't mean to create a . . ."

". . . problem? Not at all, Doctor. A difficulty, maybe."

"With . . ."

"The context."

"Context?"

"Of the text."

. . .

"Of *our* text. Here and now. Of that kind ambush of yours, to be frank."

"Ha-ha."

"Ha-ha."

"Not an ambush. Just an invitation. To a game. A game that makes one think of . . ."

"Building blocks?"

"Do you remember the first step you took? When you got here?"

"No. I don't remember taking any special steps since I got here."

"Three months ago."

"Three months . . . three years, three days, three centuries."

"After touring the hospital with the director and your wife."

"I had coffee with three other guests. Watched over by three Chinese dragons."

"In the cafe. But . . . *before* that?"

"I put away my things in my room. I'm big on putting away my—"

"But not everything fit in the closet or dresser. The books and manuscripts . . ."

"That's right. There wasn't room for them."

"So your wife suggested that . . ."

". . . they be stored in the library. It made sense. And I agreed."

"And so . . ."

"And so?"

". . . I took the liberty of looking through one of your manuscripts."

. . .

"I hope that . . ."

"No . . . No problem at—"

"As your reader. Not as your doctor."

"As *my reader?*"

"*Of your novel.* The one you gave me."

"Oh . . ."

"A signed copy, moreover. It's right there on the shelf."

"I see. I recognized it by the book's spine."

"But these manuscripts of yours . . ."

"I miss them. . . ."

. . .

"How are they? Have they sent any messages for me?"

"Who?"

"My characters. Some of them might have forgotten me. *Most, never.*"

"They're loyal?"

"You have no idea."

28

These first three months, a bit of everything had taken place. The most difficult for him had been accompanying Eva to the exit at the end of visiting hours. The idea that she was going home to an empty apartment kept worrying him—no matter how blithely she described the details of her doings, including the steps taken to move ahead with the long-deferred renovation of the apartment.

The improvements had included updating the bathrooms and kitchen, as well as a fresh coat of paint where needed. Together, they'd chosen hues that would match the reupholstered sofa and two armchairs.

Once the work was complete, he'd looked at the photos of the refurbished living room with the detachment of someone being shown images taken by relatives visiting exotic countries. He felt so removed from the scene that he wouldn't have been surprised to spot an elephant in the hallway or a Mayan pyramid on the balcony. But he hadn't failed to notice that the veranda had acquired an assortment of plants—and that the apartment, as a whole, appeared bathed in a new light. For a few seconds, he'd even heard the song of his birds. He could tell, to use one of his wife's favorite expressions, that they had seemed particularly exuberant.

He'd set aside his concerns about Eva upon seeing that she seemed to have revamped her wardrobe. And, in the still of the night, when he processed his ideas better, he'd also realized that she had changed her hairstyle.

"All you have to do now is show up here arm in arm with a new boyfriend," he'd joked.

"What about you, with your lady friend?"

"Which one?"

"The one from the cafe. And the Chinese dragons."

"Nothing that compares with your old geezer, painting the town red with you . . ."

"Geezer? He's much younger than the two of us. . . ."

Her answer had caused him to wake with a start. But then he'd chuckled a bit. And readily gone back to sleep. Because he felt good in his oasis. And it was fair that she would feel the same way. He hadn't dared to ask her what had become of his old room, fearing that the space had been transformed into the office she'd always dreamed of.

He'd allowed himself that his scale would accommodate any number of hypotheticals, as long as they were user-friendly. Such as dreams, memories, incidents, novelties that, by their very nature, wouldn't cause his ocean liners to sink. And losing his room represented a source of uncertainties he was not inclined to discuss.

At the end of that afternoon's visit, he'd said good-bye to Eva with a kiss. Before heading to the parking lot, however, she'd turned back and, sensing his unease, tried to comfort him. "What matters is that you get ready for your return. While I put the final touches on the apartment. Relax, keep up with your sessions, get better, and come back."

At first, he'd felt relieved. Then, though, he'd had second

thoughts. Something between vertigo and seduction overcame him. The truth was that going back was no longer part of his plans.

What he needed was to go *forward*.

29

If discovering the cafe with its mysterious dragons turned out to be a novelty, finding an old piano tucked away in a corner of the library had, in his view, been even more important. He hadn't noticed it when he'd come to leave his manuscripts and the handful of copies of his books. Possibly due to the solemn nature of his visit to that part of the clinic.

Having entrusted his works to someone else's hands, he felt physically distant from them for the first time. The young library attendant, aware of the significance of the gesture, had consulted the director by phone. Once his consent had been obtained, the manuscripts had been stowed on a high shelf, accessible with the aid of a ladder.

"Is it a donation?" she'd asked amiably while filling out a form.

"The books, yes," and his tone had sounded as if he were in the National Library, "but the manuscripts are merely to be held."

He'd headed back there days later. Immediately upon entering the long hallway at the end of which books, magazines, and the daily newspapers were housed, he'd heard the unmistakable sound of an out-of-tune piano. Beethoven was suffering, victim of one of the countless brutal acts committed against his legacy—in this case, *Moonlight* Sonata.

He sat in a corner without knowing who was butchering the piece, separated as he was from the sound by two bookcases. Silence having been restored shortly afterward, he grabbed an old magazine and pretended to be absorbed in reading. To his surprise, the director himself passed by his table and he had no choice but to greet him.

"I've never been able to get past the first movement of that sonata," confessed the pianist.

"Me, neither," he replied in the same modest tone.

"Do you play?"

There would have been nothing memorable about the ensuing conversation had it not been for one curious note.

"I need to play a little every morning," the director had said as he was leaving, before adding, as a heartfelt afterthought, "Otherwise, I'd go crazy."

30

"Good morning."

"Good morning, Doctor."

"How's it going today?"

"Today?"

"Yes."

"The same. Where we left off."

"May I ask a question? Nothing that . . ."

"Of course, Doctor. Anything."

"It has to do with your lack of curiosity. About my reaction . . ."

"Your reaction?"

"To your manuscripts."

"My manuscripts? Your reaction? As in *Did you like them or did you not?*"

"Not necessarily . . ."

"How so?"

"It's that the texts seem autobiographical."

"Maybe they are. Not even I know for sure, at this point. . . ."

"Full of fragments, pieces of mosaics that don't always fit together—"

"I have a weakness for digressions. As long as the sentence remains solidly in pla—"

"Except that your wife rarely puts in an appearance."

"Eva never lets herself be shown. She merely dreams."

"And that fact caught my attention."

"But dreaming isn't nothing. It can be every—"

"Which brings us to our building blocks. Why don't we start there?"

"Where?"

"With Eva."

"At that bar we first went to? The Beco da Fome?"

"Why not?"

"Eva ate four puff pastries. And I had three empanadas."

"And then?"

"The filmmaker didn't eat. He just drank."

31

He'd been saved—and this he remembered well—by his instinct. He'd protected his damsel against the advances of a dragon who, in contrast to the images embedded in the Chinese screens, had flapped his wings around Eva.

He'd acted on the spur of the moment. He was lovestruck and didn't know it.

The dragon, for his part, had proven to be kindhearted. And magnanimous. He'd sensed which of the two was bleeding. And who was merely fooling around. He'd then courteously bowed out as a contender. Better: He'd set aside his script, dimmed the lighting, and repositioned the cameras. Switching the angles of the take, he'd approached the sequence with greater sensitivity.

"Go for it," he'd even whispered on leaving the scene.

Over the course of his career, he'd written or directed a dozen memorable films, many of which the couple had watched, first at the Museum of Modern Art, then at arts cinemas and theaters in Rio de Janeiro—her eyes on the screen, his on her profile.

In the semidarkness of each of these sessions, Eva would sometimes smile at him. Then she'd squeeze his hand, as if to say, *Don't worry, I'm still here*. And he'd show a calmness that his heart kept on scrutinizing.

He'd dated, had trysts, before meeting her. He'd tested

the waters of love, but only superficially, always avoiding being swept up by the unexpected currents. And his companion, who'd simply requested a bit of black paint on a side street of a posh neighborhood, had availed herself of the clean slate breathing in front of her to set aside their political slogans for the moment.

Together, then, they'd left behind the walls of the city streets, alleys, and avenues to paint an infinite number of canvases, the force, beauty, grandeur, and integrity of which had been preserved in both their memores. And, for those who could read, between the lines of his manuscripts.

A couple like so many others. Unique only in the details.

32

"Good morning!"

"Good morning, Doctor."

"Congratulations on yesterday! I really liked it! We *all* did, very much. . . ."

"They even asked for an encore, can you believe it. . . ."

"I noticed! And everyone stayed to the end; no one left the library."

"I was a bit nervous at first. My fingers are pretty rusty. . . ."

"Hardly—a complete success! The routine here can take a toll. Not enough distraction."

"I disagree. In fact, I'd say the oppo—"

"Don't I know . . . Even the piano takes a toll."

"*Takes a toll?* The piano?"

"This stays between us, of course."

"Of course."

"When our director plays, it's always *Moonlight* Sonata. . . ."

"Actually, he's not all that bad—"

"That interminable first movement, what torture!"

"The problem is that the melody should be more legato."

"Legato?"

"The notes need to be better joined. As if the sound were continuous and flowing . . ."

"Joined? Joined how? If the man hits all the wrong keys . . ."

"But I'm gratified to have contributed to the . . ."

"We need to repeat the nighttime performance. Do it at least once a month."

"I'll see if I can brush up on my repertoire."

"No, let's stick with sambas. That's what the group likes. . . . It was great."

"Okay."

"You can repeat the same set list. . . ."

"I don't know if I'll be able to remember the or—"

"No one will notice."

"My agent would take exception to a comment like that. . . ."

"Especially coming from me! The audience member who appreciated your show more than anyone . . ."

"Really?"

"I kept imagining you playing in bars. Young, shoulder-length hair . . ."

"Good times . . . I was part of a trio."

"I know! It's all in your manu—"

"My fellow musicians moved on. I was the only one left behind."

"Fortunately for us. Next time we need to invite your wife."

"Eva?"

"No?"

"All right. But then . . ."

"Then?"

"I'll play with my eyes wide shut. . . . And we'll see what the gods will!"

33

The psychiatrist had indicated that he'd like to increase their number of sessions. From two to three times a week, the doctor had suggested.

For his part, he hesitated. Feeling encroached upon, as well as hemmed in by interferences, he knew exactly where certain discussions tended to end up. And this right when his life was going so well . . . *Why couldn't they just leave him alone?*

He'd complained to Eva. She'd kept quiet but then gone back to the topic of his returning to the apartment. Leading him to make a remark of questionable taste: "At least here my window is on the ground floor."

It was his way of defending himself. With language. But it created a sense of unease.

The insistence on *making progress* hung in the air among the three of them. What seemed to be in play was "an outcome." Or rather, getting somewhere. In Eva's case, the apartment. In the doctor's, to a discharge deserving of pats on the back.

But how? If not even in his texts did he feel obligated to *get somewhere*? How to deal with something as ineffable as progress?

Ineffable. . . . Funny, that was how Eva had referred to one of his first texts. . . . At the time, the word had left him anxious, for all that it implied of the unknown.

And now, on top of this, he no longer knew how to avoid the challenges that besieged him.

Until the morning he'd once again reached for language in search of protection. When he'd availed himself of a romantic vision of the doctor's ("Love is there; it's just buried beneath the thousands of pages of your manuscripts") to use a word he never would have resorted to under normal circumstances:

"To discuss the issue, Doctor, would be the equivalent of exhuming it."

He hadn't said "resurrecting" it. And now the unburied corpse stood between them.

34

His old filmmaker friend would say that he was bleeding. As had happened at the Beco da Fome, when he'd seen his love threatened. And his friend would have been right: He was suffering in his oasis. Lost yet again amid wishes that disregarded his own.

Everyone wanted to *cure him* at any cost. As had been the case with his nonsensical childhood monologues and the puzzling silences of his adolescence.

An odd feeling . . . because his surroundings and routine bolstered him, from the serene safety of his anonymous room to the simple beauty of his bench beneath the tree, from coffee hours in the cafe with new friends to the moments alone at the piano. Beyond that, having stopped writing had unburdened him of a weight that he'd carried for years. He could now concentrate on living.

At the same time, he was aware that something unfamiliar loomed. Except that he couldn't quite define it. Inevitably, he would end up thinking about his demise. A prospect that didn't worry him in the least. As no invitation had been extended for Death to visit his oasis.

Then what? *Madness?* As if insanity hadn't been his close companion for so long, responsible for the joy he still managed to tap into around him . . .

He could have discussed these issues with his filmmaker friend, who had been there for him at the beginning. On the cusp of something that might not even have happened. And that, upon coming to light, had given meaning to his existence.

A fleeting existence, all things considered, but fleeting or not, *his*—and no one else's.

The filmmaker, who today surely wouldn't even remember him, much less the small scene shared with a very young couple more than fifty years ago at a bar long since gone, had all the necessary credentials to understand him. Besides being sensitive, he'd behaved like a gentleman. A prince worthy of Visconti and Lampedusa.

But if he now went back to that bygone episode—if his recollections were becoming repetitive and starting to drift, as had once happened to one of his texts—it was because the grounding cables that had helped keep him tethered were finally beginning to come undone.

And that did worry him.

Nothing that a strong rope, tied to a branch of his tree within reach, couldn't solve. Hadn't the heads of the hospital made sure to choose a ground-floor room for him? With a window overlooking the garden?

He considered his options. With an eye for the details.

It would be snowing that fateful night. . . . An unprecedented occurrence in a city known for its tropical climate. Supportive, nature would reinvent herself, creating a backdrop on a par with the last enigma of his life. As a result, the old almond tree, and the carpet of grass beneath it, would be blanketed in white.

In the early-morning hours, on his way to his out-of-tune piano, the hospital director would imagine that he was dreaming as he came upon a landscape both strange and familiar. His shock would increase upon realizing that he didn't even feel cold. And was actually perspiring. A few feet above his head, he'd hear the song of birds, before noticing that several of them hopped amid the foliage, affectionately pecking at the disheveled hair of a blue-and-purple pianist.

He smiled to himself. . . . However poetic and evocative these scenes turned out, they were no more than fantasies. Worthy, at most, of one of his imaginary trunks. And, today, fantasies no longer appealed to him.

He didn't seek easy solutions, which echoed former weaknesses—subjecting Eva, moreover, to unnecessary sadness. What's more, he'd chosen life. Let Death knock on someone else's door.

That said, what other options remained?

To sail out to sea through unknown waters. Surrendering himself to currents that still took interest in him.

He paused for a long moment. And then it slowly dawned on him that the best thing that could have happened to his manuscripts had been their successive rejection by all publishers.

Seeing his texts come out as books would have meant losing them, letting go of their stories. They would have been tied and bound up forever. Read by strangers, they'd be appropriated by them, giving rise to musings, reflections, opinions. Leaving him powerless, outside his plots, as if a border—this time impermeable—separated them.

Now, in contrast, his manuscripts belonged to him and no one else.

He could alter them indefinitely, reopening doors that would lead to all kinds of scenarios, so that new characters could step into a scene; or padlocking them closed, without giving satisfaction to whomever.

To think that he owed to Eva the suggestion to store his

texts at the library . . . Could she have seen the clear path that lay ahead of him?

It was his, the promised land—to which he would dedicate the final years of his life.

35

"How'd it go?"

"The conversation with your doctor? It went well. He was hesitant but ended up agreeing."

"To putting off my sessions?"

"Yes. For two weeks."

"I would've preferred canceling for good."

"He has no way of doing that. Hospital protocol assumes . . ."

". . . *that the treatment is part of the healing process.*"

"And neither he nor you can give up that proto—"

"I know, Eva, the doctor told me. He's not a bad person. Just stubborn."

They'd walked through the garden toward his tree. At that hour of the morning, their usual bench was still free. They settled in the shade of the almond tree.

"Beautiful, this tree of mine, isn't it? And what luck that the bedroom window looks out on it. Sometimes, at night, I leave the curtains parted so I can watch the foliage dance on the ceiling. The choreographies are never the same."

"And the music? Contrast or counterpoint?"

They continued in close harmony. Everything might change, except the complicity they shared.

"Total contrast! Traditional opera arias, 'Nessun Dorma,' 'O mio babbino caro,' competing with dissonant choreographies, leading nature to dance with abandon beneath a dizzying sea of stars . . ."

"I wouldn't be able to close my eyes all night. . . ."

"Neither can I—I go back to my texts and stay there. . . . I've reached some unbelievable conclusions. . . ."

"The texts left at the library?"

"Those and others. Along with their countless rivals, which keep showing up. Hieroglyphs generating spirals of energy, words moving ideas through unexplored spaces, sentences that make sense until the moment they turn against one another . . ."

"As in a game of building blocks?"

For a few minutes, they remained in silence, contemplating the foliage that, stirred by the breeze, fluttered just above their heads. Listening to the birds' song without actually seeing them evoked memories of their years together in their cozy old apartment.

It wasn't the first time they'd spent a moment together on that bench. It was, however, the first since he'd made the decision to return to the voyages of his childhood. When the *cargo-hold baggage*—his father's designation for the trunks to embark prior to their own boarding time—awaited the porters coming for them in the entry hall. While the *cabin baggage*—which would travel in their spacious stateroom and included his suitcase with a few toys—waited in the parlor along with their coats.

What seas and oceans might they be crossing now?

These were times of leave-taking, each member of the family wrapped up with his or her final routines, his father separating passports and traveler's checks, or making one last phone call to some colleague from the diplomatic corps; his mother collecting the books she'd read on board or adjusting her hat in front of the mirror; and he wandering around the house stripped of furnishings he wouldn't see for a while, running from one corner to another, astride two worlds but insecure in both, always putting on a brave face while making every effort to pretend not to miss what would be left behind—and even less so the friends he'd made during those two years, a relatively short stopover already relegated to his past. Because other friends would come along, as his parents assured him, and, after those, others still. There was no reason for tears.

He was already a young man.

Except that he knew, from previous experiences, that he'd never return to that home or that city. Worse: Were he to go back, he wouldn't be the same, nor would the city come close to the one preserved in his memory.

And he'd face a desolate space, a wasteland.

Maybe this accounted for the particular kind of sadness he experienced, similar to that he now noticed on Eva's face. As if, on his bench beneath the tree, she, too, was in search of words that would help him confront that strange mix of losses and conquests.

"And then?" she whispered.

And then . . .

It would be up to him to inject life into something that, for the time being, still waited in the wings. He thought that, as in the past, he would manage to make the alchemy work, and, with any luck, come up with the perfect synthesis—one that would let the story be told.

The hour of truth had perhaps finally arrived.

"And then, Eva . . . *the future.*"

"The future? And what is it you see in our future?"

"A long trip."

"We're going on a trip?"

"We are."

"Where to?"

"Far away, very far away. An adventure that might last years, many years . . . Fourteen, if we are lucky."

"Wonderful! And what else can you see, sweetheart?"

Sweetheart . . . It had been years since she'd used that language. Not for lack of affection. That had never been lacking. Even during his bouts of uncertainty or depression, Eva had never abandoned him to his own fate.

Words, he now realized, had lost some of their power, becoming delicate and then tainted by their fragility. Having changed ever so slightly, they had replaced one another, burying, in the process, the ones needed most. Like the example just revived with the tenderness of a caress: *sweetheart*.

"What else can I see, Eva?"

She was the only audience he would ever need. And he wouldn't miss a single note. With a light heart once again, he spread his arms, as if he were the conductor of a grand orchestra, and set off on his inner saga.

"The docks, the moored ship, the three stacks giving off smoke, people laughing, people crying, handkerchiefs and confetti blowing in the wind, passengers slowly climbing the gangways, the van parked with our cargo-hold baggage, the porters keeping busy, my father on edge, checking for our trunks and suitcases, not forgetting the hatbox, my mother bent over me, buttoning up my wool coat because of the cold wind, the little coat with that ridiculous cap . . ."

"And smothering you with kisses? So you wouldn't be sad?"

"And smothering me with kisses. So I wouldn't be sad."

"Another departure?"

"Yes."

There would be many days, many nights. And awaiting them on the other side of the world, a new language, with new slang, new texts, new labyrinths, new stories.

Except that he'd no longer step on eggshells. As if by magic, he'd find the means to repair his canoe and, embracing Eva, brave the four winds of the seas and oceans he had yet to face. . . .

Life was beautiful.

Could this be why his wife's look now conveyed such confidence and hope? Lines and drawings of all kinds of shapes and colors emerged from the horizon, as if already welcoming him at his new destination, a place covered with sketches and a mysterious choice of words, some written, some painted, others crossed out, erased, barely visible, and all essentially strange. . . .

But all alive and within his reach. Waiting for him in the still of the night . . .

Waiting for them.

Edgard Telles Ribeiro, recipient of Brazil's most prestigious literary prizes, including the Jabuti Prize, Brazilian Academy of Letters Prize, and Brazilian PEN Club Prize, is the author of fourteen works of fiction including *The Impostor* and *As If by Magic*. He studied cinema at University of California, Los Angeles, worked as a film critic for several newspapers before becoming a career diplomat, and is a member of the Brazilian Academy of Letters. He lives in New York and Rio de Janeiro.

Kim M. Hastings is a freelance translator and editor. She lived in São Paulo for several years, studied Brazilian language and literature at Brown University, and holds a PhD in Spanish and Portuguese from Yale. Her translations include Edgard Telles Ribeiro's award-winning novel *His Own Man* and novellas of *The Impostor* and *As If by Magic*, as well as shorter fiction, poetry, and interviews of other Brazilian authors. She lives in Connecticut.

Margaret A. Neves holds an MA in English and Linguistics from Colorado State University. While living in Salvador, Brazil, she translated works into English for several Brazilian authors, including Lygia Fagundes Telles, Jorge Amado, and Moacyr Scliar. She is also the translator of one of Edgard Telles Ribeiro's novellas in *The Impostor* and three of his short stories in *As If by Magic*. She lives in Colorado.

Bellevue Literary Press is devoted to publishing literary fiction and nonfiction at the intersection of the arts and sciences because we believe that science and the humanities are natural companions for understanding the human experience. We feature exceptional literature that explores the nature of consciousness, embodiment, and the underpinnings of the social contract. With each book we publish, our goal is to foster a rich, interdisciplinary dialogue that will forge new tools for thinking and engaging with the world.

To support our press and its mission, and for our full catalogue of published titles, please visit us at blpress.org.

Bellevue Literary Press
New York